Broken

Some things can never be fixed

Given a choice between slavery and ostracization, Jessica chooses to kneel naked before her department head so she can continue studying for her PhD in psychology. That decision takes her down a dark path to abuse, exploitation, and torment of both her body and her spirit.

Korin I. Dushayl "writes with authority and compassion about those who live within the lifestyle. Broken and Shattered explore issues including finding and initiating a submissive partner, informed consent, and the difference between dominating someone and exploiting their needs."

Elizabeth Coldwell
author, anthologist, magazine editor

As a FemDom, I.G. Frederick knows first hand the beauty of symbiotic D/s relationships filled with love. As an observer she sees the many ways BDSM turns ugly. She writes about abusive and tragic interactions as Korin I. Dushayl.

I.G. Frederick trades words for cash, specializing in erotic and transgressive fiction and poetry since 2001. Her erotic short

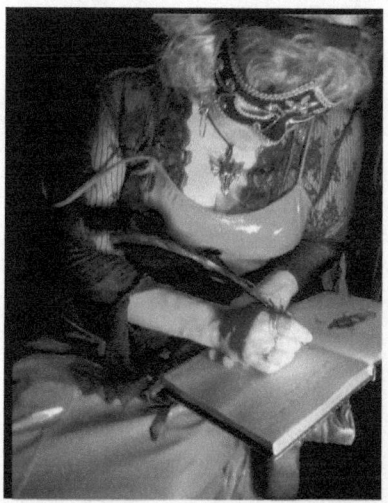 stories appeared in Hustler Fantasies, Forum, Foreplay, and Desire Presents, as well as electronic, audio, and print anthologies. Her novels receive high praise from readers, critics, and other authors.

Ms. Frederick, owns the man she adores who although dominant in the rest of his life, demonstrates his love by serving as her submissive.

http://transgressivewriter.com

BROKEN

Some things can never be fixed

Korin I. Dushayl

Author of *Shattered* and *Playing With Dolls*

Broken
Second Edition
© 2011 by I.G. Frederick

ISBN: 978-1-937471-91-0

Pussy Cat Press
http://pussycatpress.com/publisher.html/
P.O. Box 19764
Portland OR 97280

First published in the U.S.A. 2008

Dedication

To my best friend, confidante, and proofreader/
editor, Cindy, who helps me keep an even keel
as I navigate the waters of life's journey.

Chapter One

Jessica Richards picked her way through the wet grass, trying to keep the heels of her Louis Vuitton boots from sinking into the turf. She made her way to the gaping hole next to her mother's grave, clutching a silk handkerchief she could use to dab at her eyes and prevent tears from streaking her makeup. When she finally reached the graveside, the fake grass under the canopy allowed her to stop tiptoeing.

The moment she took her seat and crossed her long legs, a short, balding man in a cheap raincoat and worn, mud-spattered loafers spoke. "Dearly beloved, we gather today to mourn the passing of," he paused to check a piece of paper tucked into his prayer book. "Francis 'Frank' Richards, devoted husband and father." With that last word, he looked at Jessica with an expression he probably intended as sympathetic, but that set her teeth on edge. She had never seen the man before and he had no clue what kind of man her father had been.

For the past several days, she had endured condolences tinged with scorn from anyone who read the news reports about the well-known investor found by his housekeeper with a pistol in his hand and a bullet in his brain. Jessica shut out the Reverend's deep, sonorous voice, focusing instead on the leather scent of her trench coat, the softness of its cashmere lining against her skin, and the drip of the rain on the canvas tent above the plastic folding chairs.

When he finally finished droning on, Jessica stood and stepped closer to the polished mahogany casket adorned with a spray of white lilies. She put her leather gloves in front of her lips, careful not to smudge her lipstick, and touched the casket. An errant tear trickled down her cheek and her handkerchief came away with a black smudge from her mascara.

Jessica pressed her lips together and stepped away. Walking back to the limousine, she could hear the creak of the gears as the grave diggers lowered the casket into the ground. The thunk as it came to rest at the bottom of the concrete vault reminded her that losing both her parents before her twenty-third birthday would define the rest of her life. She pressed the handkerchief below both eyes, hoping to avoid additional smears.

Before she climbed into the Town Car, Jessica looked around at the meager turnout. Only her father's attorney, Louis Foster, her friend Alyssa Volker, a few of her father's associates, and the housekeeper had braved the drizzly September morning to venture just north of Chicago to Graceland Cemetery. Dozens more had turned out for her mother's funeral a year ago. But Lenora Richards' life had ended in a fiery crash on the Edens Expressway, rather than at her own hand.

Except for Louis, everyone hurried to their own cars, sparing Jessica additional platitudes. Louis followed her into the Town Car and rode back to the house with her. Although he didn't speak, he held her gloved hand in both of his bare ones.

Just before the car pulled into the long, circular driveway of the house on Lake Shore Drive, Jessica swallowed hard. Although she had known him since childhood, she had no clue how to open a discussion about her finances with her father's attorney. She closed her eyes. That conversation, she supposed, could wait. Now, she needed to play hostess if anyone insisted on prolonging the funeral by visiting the house.

Fumbling in her Versace handbag, Jessica found her compact. To her dismay, despite her choice of a waterproof formula, her tears had created a ring of mascara around her green eyes. In addition, the rain had frizzed her normally straight black hair. Knowing she couldn't do anything about her hair without gel and a dryer, she moistened her handkerchief with her tongue and tried to scrub some of the black mess from the pale skin under her dark lashes.

J

When the battered pickup truck finally pulled away, Jessica eased her blue Mercedes-Benz convertible into a metered spot in front of the dingy coffee shop on Halsted Street. She put the car in park, turned off the engine, and gripped the steering wheel until her hands stopped shaking. After ignoring her phone calls for the past three weeks, Louis had finally had his secretary summon Jessica to meet him in this horrid neighborhood. Jessica took a deep breath, climbed out of the car, and used the clicker to set the alarm.

She hesitated before pushing open the door to the coffee shop, wondering if the secretary had given her the wrong address. Then she saw Louis huddled in a booth at the back of the restaurant, his hands wrapped around a chipped coffee mug.

"Whatever possessed you to select this dump as a meeting place?" Jessica asked, sliding onto the plastic seat across the stained melamine table.

"Get used to it. This is the best you can afford these days." He practically spat the words out.

Jessica stared at Louis Foster's lined face, pale against

black hair trimmed above his ears, with gray streaks at his temples. She had always thought of him as more like an uncle than her father's attorney, and his tone stung as much as his words confused her.

A busty, pink-uniformed waitress approached the table, a coffee pot in one hand. At least a size fourteen, Jessica thought with scorn.

"You want coffee, honey?"

"I don't suppose you can serve me a mocha?"

Louis turned the cup in front of Jessica over. "She'll have regular joe, just like me."

The waitress filled Jessica's cup. "Anything else?"

"Thanks, no," Louis said.

Jessica found a dish of plastic creamer containers next to the metal napkin holder under the grimy window. She emptied two into her cup and poured in sugar from the metal-topped dispenser. "You going to tell me what's going on?"

He waved his hand across the table. "Isn't it obvious? You're broke."

"Louis, please stop kidding around." Jessica took a sip and grimaced. "This stuff is awful."

"Unless you've got someone to buy you better coffee, you're going to have to learn to live with it. And without credit cards. I've had to cancel all the ones your father gave you as of this morning."

Jessica tightened her grip on the coffee cup until the heat penetrating the ceramic hurt her hand.

"Your father spoiled you rotten, despite my advice to let you learn how to survive on your own. Well, he and the money are gone — you have no one to give you credit cards or pay all your bills. You need to make your own car and insurance payments or sell it. You'll have to come up with rent, groceries. No one will take care of you anymore." Louis stared at the liquid in his cup.

Jessica's looked inside her own coffee cup. It looked like a latte but tasted like dirt. Unable to comprehend his anger and bitterness toward her, she tried to at least make sense of Louis' words. "How am I supposed to pay my rent? I've got at least five more years of graduate school before I can expect any kind of income. My father promised to pay for my education. I could see him setting up a trust to make sure I finished school, but surely he made allowances for living expenses as well?"

Louis looked up at her. Dark shadows rimmed his brown eyes. "Your parents already paid for four years of college and carried you for the past three years of graduate school. With what they've shelled out already, you'd think you could get some kind of job. There's no trust fund. If you want to continue graduate school, you'll have to figure out how to pay the tuition. You're busted."

"You keep saying that. What do you mean?" Jessica lifted the cup to her lips, sniffed it, and set it back down. Louis seemed angry at her and she had no idea why.

"You do know why your father ate his own gun?"

"He finally succumbed to grief for my mother."

Louis snorted. "Surely you get some exposure to the outside world from your hallowed academic halls. Haven't you paid any attention to what's going on in the stock market?"

Jessica shook her head. Her father had repeatedly told her to concentrate on her studies and not worry about money — that he would always take care of her. She had never held a job, written a check, or filled out a credit card application.

"Well, I'll make it simple then: he lost everything. All the volatile high tech stock he invested in tanked." Louis picked up his cup, drained it, and plunked it down on the table. "You're destitute." The cold, unemotional way he spoke those words punched Jessica in the gut. She almost wanted the anger back. "The house is on the market, but with real estate prices where they are and all the stuff your parents added that no one will pay for, you'll be lucky to get enough to pay off the mortgage."

Jessica blinked rapidly to keep her tears at bay. "But what about the money from Mom's estate?"

"Gone. All you've inherited is debt."

"How could you let this happen? My father promised to support me while I worked on my PhD. I'm having a hard enough time with the course work and my thesis as it is — I'll never make it if I have to get a job."

Louis shrugged. "Then I guess you'll have to quit." He sighed and his voice softened. "Look, Jessica, I didn't let this happen. I've been struggling for the past three weeks trying to figure out where all the money went. I can't even find enough to pay off your father's debts. And, given the state of his affairs, I've essentially been working for free." He ran his fingers through his hair. "I warned him about ..." He shook his head as if trying to clear his head. "Doesn't matter now."

Jessica stared at him, afraid that if she tried to speak she would burst into tears.

"Sorry, hon." Louis reached across the table and patted Jessica's hand. "I know this is hard for you to accept, that's why I dragged you down here so the reality would sink in. You need to understand sooner, rather than later, the gravity of your financial situation or you're just going to get yourself in a world of trouble. I've tried to straighten out the mess your father left, but I just can't afford to help you anymore."

Louis slid out of the booth, stood, and tossed three one dollar bills on the table. "Coffee's on me, but you're on your own now. Gotta go." He walked out the front door before Jessica could decide if she wanted him to come back.

The waitress stepped up to the table with the coffee pot in her hand. "Ya want a refill, sugar?" She grabbed the money and stuck it in the pocket of her apron.

Jessica didn't look up. The waitress represented everything she didn't want in her life: double-digit dress size, cheap clothing, menial job, no education. "No, thanks." She waited until the waitress' white sneakers disappeared from view, put her elbows on the table, and buried her face in her hands. Her shoulders shook, but she managed, except when she gasped for air, to keep her sobs silent.

J

Jessica unlocked the mailbox in the foyer of her apartment and pulled out envelope after envelope. They all had yellow stickers with her address printed on them plastered over the plastic windows showing the address of the now-empty house on Lake Shore Drive. She had gotten out of the habit of checking her mailbox regularly, since all of the bills went to her father and most of the rest of her mail consisted of credit card offers and flyers from nearby stores. I bet no one will offer me credit cards now.

Once inside her apartment, she sat down at her desk and stared at the pile of envelopes. Hands shaking, she reached for the Samurai sword letter opener and sliced through the top of the first one. Her three-hundred-eighty-five-a-month car payment, ten days late, required an additional fifty-dollar penalty. Monthly insurance premiums for the car cost a hundred-and-forty dollars. Those two payments alone were almost as much as her rent.

Jessica dropped the letter opener on the pile of unopened envelopes and rested her chin on her open palms. The pile included bills for telephone, cell, electricity, cable television, Internet, and credit cards. She had no idea how much her tuition payments were or if they had been paid for this term.

Those bills also had always gone directly to her father.

She picked up the late notice for her car payment. If she sold the car for enough to pay off the loan, she would eliminate that payment as well as insurance, gasoline, and parking costs. Jessica slid the pile of bills into a flat row and picked out the American Express and Visa envelopes. Without money to spend downtown or out in Schaumburg at the mall, would it really matter if she didn't have transportation? She set those two envelopes, unopened, on top of the bill from the insurance company.

Rifling through the bills from the utility companies, she added the phone bill to the pile of suddenly unnecessary expenses. She would rather give that up than her cell. The cable television bill got added to the I-can-live-without-it pile. The bill for broadband Internet stayed with the electric and cell phone envelopes — giving that up would make research more difficult. One by one, she opened the bills and entered the amounts into a spreadsheet on her computer.

Even with all her sacrifices — giving up car, telephone, cable, and shopping — Jessica didn't see how she could manage on less than eight hundred a month plus whatever she needed for tuition and books. One elbow on the black lacquered desktop, she leaned her forehead on the heel of her palm and stared at the computer screen. She would have to work full-time to earn enough to cover basic living expenses and tuition. "How the hell am I supposed to find time to keep up with school if I have to put in forty hours a week at some menial job?" Neither the computer nor the stack of bills offered an answer.

A tear rolled down her cheek, and Jessica caught it with the back of her hand. Her father's death threatened to destroy everything she had worked so hard on for the past three years. With a doctorate in psychology, she planned to make a name for herself in academic circles, doing cutting edge research on depression.

Jessica let loose a string of expletives and immediately covered her mouth, grateful no one could hear her cursing her father for not making more sensible investments. She closed her eyes, remembering when he quit his job to concentrate on day trading. She would come home from school to hear him brag about making thousands of dollars in the stock market in a single day. Her weekends at home invariably led to shopping excursions with her mother. Reveling in their new luxurious lifestyle, Lenora introduced Jessica to designer fashion, high-end furniture, exotic foods and more.

Pushing away from her desk and her memories, Jessica looked around at the black leather sofa and chairs, the carved, lacquered tables, brass lamps, and Bose sound system. She had acquired most of the hand-carved, Asian-style furniture since her mother missed a curve at a hundred and sixty miles an hour and crashed her new Ferrari into a concrete wall. The high-end furniture, designer shoes, and new jewelry hadn't closed the hole in Jessica's life that her mother left behind. Still, though they provided no solace for her grief, she had become rather accustomed to luxuries. And even if she readjusted to a more plebeian lifestyle, she still had no way of supporting herself.

Chapter Two

"I'm afraid I have all the T.A.s and R.A.s that I need for this term, Jessica." Professor Bob Clement leaned back in the large purple chair that barely held his impressive girth. The man stood six foot, four inches tall and his belly spilled over his thighs when he sat. "You should have come to me at the beginning of the term. I would have liked to have you on the team. The work you've done on your thesis shows a keen understanding of the role neurotransmitters play in triggering chronic depression." He brought the chair back down so he could fold his hands together on his office supply store desk calendar. "Besides, I thought you had the means to finance your education without subsidies from the University."

"I thought so, too." Jessica wanted to slip off her leather pumps and rub her tired toes. It had taken her nearly forty-five minutes to walk from her apartment. The brisk autumn wind had turned her cheeks red and made her nose runny. She resisted sniveling. "But my circumstances have changed rather drastically."

Professor Clement pulled on his black beard speckled with grey. "Most faculty select the students who will work for them during the fall term in the summer. The only person who might, and I empathize might, be in a position to add a student is the department chair."

Jessica cringed. That creep?

"And, while I wouldn't recommend that you change advisors this late in the process, if you need financial assistance, Professor Lawrence may be your only option for getting onboard as an assistant." He leaned his forearms on the desk. "Shame, really. Your interests have dovetailed so nicely with my research. I'll write you a nice recommendation, of course." He chewed on his lower lip. "Not that my support will carry much weight with Lawrence."

He stood up, towering over Jessica even when she rose to her full five feet, nine inches. "Whatever you decide, I wish you the very best." He extended a hand.

Jessica limped out of his cluttered office and leaned against the wall in the hallway outside his now-closed door. Just the thought of trudging back home made her feet ache from her toes to her heels.

When she finally arrived back at her apartment, Jessica indulged in a hot bath both to soak away the pain in her feet and give herself time to think. With lavender-scented steam filling the tub enclosure, she let the heat take the tension out of her shoulders and the ache from her legs. She probably needed to adjust her wardrobe if walking to school became part of her daily routine. Once the Chicago winter set in, she would need to forgo her designer skirts and jackets for warm pants and coat. And she definitely needed to look through her shoe collection for a more comfortable pair to walk in.

Her cell phone rang, and Jessica slid the glass door open just enough to retrieve it from the stool next to the tub. Alyssa had tried to reach her every day since the funeral and Jessica had let the calls go to voice mail. She took a deep breath of steam-heated air and tried to make her voice sound cheerful. "Hey, Alyssa."

"How are you doing, dear?" Perhaps because of the difference in their ages, Alyssa tended to treat Jessica more like a beloved niece than a college friend.

"Considering switching advisors." Jessica sighed and

closed the enclosure so no more of the heat would escape.

"Whatever for, dear? Haven't you had enough stress to deal with?"

Jessica shrugged causing the bath water to ripple. "Professor Clement can't take on another research assistant and since my father died, I'm a little short of funds."

"But, I thought you chose him specifically because his areas of research matched your interests so nicely."

Jessica chewed on her lip. Professor Clement had heartily approved of her thesis topic and they had already discussed possible dissertation subjects. Professor Lawrence hadn't done any work at all in the efficacy of pharmacological treatment with and without therapy for depressive patients. "Yeah, but now I'm thinking I might be better off going into private practice."

"What? You love doing research." Alyssa made a noise that sounded rather like a snort. "How will you have time for that if you're seeing patients all day?"

"Academia doesn't pay. Without Dad's financial backing, I'm not sure I'm willing to make the necessary sacrifices." A week with no credit cards or vehicle had caused Jessica to seriously reconsider her career aspirations. The Mercedes-Benz convertible she had returned to the dealer three days ago cost more than she could hope to earn in a year as an assistant professor. Designer clothing and shoes filled her closet and before Louis Foster's devastating news, she hadn't prepared a meal for herself in months.

"No inheritance?"

Jessica shook her head, even though she realized Alyssa couldn't see it. "Nothing but debt."

"Oh." Alyssa must have figured out the connection between Jessica's father's death and her new financial woes. Jessica rolled her eyes.

"I'll be okay. I'm eliminating all but the necessary expenses. If I can get a research assistant's position I'll manage until I graduate." Jessica's voice caught. "Listen, I'm in the tub and I probably shouldn't be talking on the phone. Call you later?"

"Let's do lunch."

"Sure." Jessica disconnected the call, set the phone outside, and sank back into her bath water. Telling Alyssa made it all seem more real. Giving up her accustomed comforts while she completed graduate school seemed manageable. But the thought of living frugally unless or until she reached full professor made Jessica weep. Her sobbing caused her to lose her breath. She slid open the glass door to let out steam and gasp in fresh air.

When her hands stopped shaking, Jessica pulled the stopper, stood up, and slicked water off her skin enjoying the feel of her flat tummy, large firm breasts, and narrow hips. She reached for the Egyptian cotton bath sheet.

Private practice had never appealed to her, until now. With the right connections, she could earn six figures within a year or two of getting her PhD. Professor Clement definitely would not provide the right connections for that. While well-known in academic circles, he had no standing among private practitioners. Professor William Lawrence, on the other hand, had a reputation for making his students' careers in both academia and private practice.

After drying off, Jessica wrapped her wet hair in a fluffy towel and pulled a dusty pink silk charmeuse robe around her. Could she tolerate working with Lawrence through the years it would take to complete her dissertation? Padding out to her computer in her bare feet, she logged onto the Internet. Jessica cringed when she read Lawrence's page on the University website. He specialized in sexual risk-taking behaviors, sexual assault, therapeutic recovery following trauma, treatment of PTSD, panic disorder, and other anxiety disorders.

She put a hand on the thick manila folder next to the keyboard that held notes from her thesis research on neurotransmitters and how they responded to drug and other therapy. For her dissertation, she had planned to widen her study of brain function as it related to mental disorders. Lawrence's research into the impact of trauma on mental health would lead her off in a different direction. How would his fields of study serve her if she intended to go into private practice? She unwrapped the towel and rubbed her shoulder-length black hair dry, tossed the towel at the hamper in the bedroom and ran her long, lacquered fingers through the strands to untangle them.

She sat back down at her desk and pulled a yellow legal pad from one of the slots in the matching hutch that held her computer monitor. Drawing a line down the middle, she wrote "Pro" at the top of one column and "Con" at the top of the other. First in the Pro list: as department head, Professor Lawrence probably could take on another graduate student if he chose. At the top of the Con list: he repulsed her. However, his leadership had contributed to the prestige that had convinced her to apply to Chicago University's graduate school. She added that to the Pro list.

And, at least if she signed on with Lawrence, she didn't have to start over. She had completed the research on her thesis and had written two thirds of it. The subject didn't fall into Lawrence's area of expertise, but Jessica imagined she could still get Clement to sign off on it. Since she had only started thinking about what topic she wanted to tackle for her dissertation, finding a subject area that Professor Lawrence would appreciate wouldn't require her to throw out work she had already done.

She took a deep breath and dove into the abstracts of Lawrence's published work that she could find online. An hour later, Jessica rubbed her eyes and added another topic to the Con list on her sheet. None of Lawrence's areas of expertise interested her.

Jessica decided to try a different tack. She searched

for students who had written their dissertation under Lawrence's auspices. Although she couldn't find anyone still living in the Chicago area, the collective resumes she uncovered lengthened the Pro column significantly: Steven Billing, professor of psychology at Stanford; Rita Zolan, who apparently earned almost as much in speaking fees as she did from her Boston practice; Lynette Johnson, a professor at the University of Washington with papers published in every professional journal Jessica had ever read. All had achieved the level of success she hoped to find, building prestigious or lucrative careers.

Lawrence certainly seemed to have accomplished both. He lived near the University off Sheridan Drive in one of Chicago's pricier neighborhoods. She had seen him driving both a brand new Acura sedan and a BMW Z3. He always wore designer suits and she had heard stories about lavish parties at New Year's and Graduation for faculty and selected students.

Jessica tried to find out how he could afford all of that on a Department Head's salary. She could find no record of well-paid speaking engagements or research fellowships. He didn't have a private practice and saw no patients. Jessica hated not having enough information. Although she didn't really have seventy-five dollars to spare for a comprehensive background check, she decided she needed the information more than she needed the groceries that money would buy.

The background check didn't offer any answers and Jessica cursed the cost. Scanning the pages, she only learned that Lawrence had no debt except his mortgage and, given the value of his house, that seemed small. The report included no evidence of family money. She knew he rarely traveled and searching winners lists, she found no record of him winning large sums of money or even small ones on the river boats in the Mississippi River or the Indian casinos in Wisconsin. She just could not imagine him dealing drugs or conceive of any other way for him to afford his opulent lifestyle on a professor's salary.

Jessica looked at the two columns on the legal pad. Even though the Pros now exceeded the Cons, she still had serious doubts about approaching Lawrence to be her advisor. Then, she underlined each of his former student's names that she had written down. More than anything else, she wanted access to the advantages Lawrence's approval apparently bestowed upon his protégés.

Chapter Three

Jessica straightened her skirt and hefted the portfolio containing the work to which she had devoted the past week. Normally she would have spent a month or more pulling together notes, outlining her research parameters and expectations, studying Lawrence's publications. But she needed to pay her rent in nine days. She knocked on Lawrence's door.

His office was twice as big as Clement's with much more luxurious furnishings. A polished mahogany desk stood in front of the large window looking out onto the quad. Two leather, wingback chairs faced the desk and Jessica estimated the chair behind it cost more than two-thousand dollars. Floor-to-ceiling bookcases, also mahogany, filled with reference volumes, textbooks, and professional journals lined the walls.

Although he had told her to enter, Professor Lawrence ignored Jessica and continued scribbling notes on a student's paper with a gold and black Montblanc fountain pen. He had a light brown fringe of hair surrounding an oily pate and watery, brown eyes behind Berkshire Chase spectacles. Short and dumpy, he wore a charcoal grey Hugo Boss suit, a French blue dress shirt with two-thousand dollar gold knot cufflinks and a silk tie that probably cost more than she had paid for six months of car insurance.

Jessica moved the portfolio from under one arm to in front

of her chest and back. She cleared her throat. She checked her watch at least four times.

Finally, after fifteen minutes, Professor Lawrence looked up. "What do you need?"

Jessica cleared her throat again and gripped her portfolio tighter, trying to keep her hands from shaking. "I wanted to speak with you about a research assistant position."

"Why would you come to me? I'm not your advisor."

"I was hoping to change that." Jessica shifted from one foot to the other. "May I sit down?"

Lawrence raised one eyebrow and glared at her. Jessica remained standing.

"I brought a draft of my dissertation proposal with me and I hoped you would review it and consider taking me on."

"Isn't Clement your advisor?" Lawrence put his hands behind his head and leaned back in his chair. "Why aren't you discussing this with him?"

"Because after completing the research for my thesis, I decided I would rather get involved in some of the work you're doing. Also, I really need a research assistant position so I can afford to continue my studies. Professor Clement doesn't have any opportunities available."

"And what makes you think I do? You should have applied for an R.A. position last summer."

Jessica lowered her eyes. He would expect deference."Yes, I know," she whispered. "But I had an abrupt and unexpected change in my financial circumstances."

"Which is my problem, why?"

He didn't have to attack her for asking. "It's not, sir. I only hoped that you would find the research proposal that I've prepared of enough interest to make it worth your while to allow me to stay in school." And have a place to live next month.

Lawrence pulled a file folder from a pile on the corner of

his desk. He opened it and Jessica recognized her student records. "You've never pulled better than a B average. You barely passed your Comps." Lawrence shook his head. "I only accept outstanding students and you've done nothing better than mediocre." He flipped through the pages in the folder. "The hypothesis that you built your thesis on is flawed." He jabbed at the document with his index finger. "Most of these therapies are no better than snake oil and hocus pocus. And your methodology is questionable at best, fraudulent at worst."

Jessica dropped into one of the wingback chairs, biting her lip to keep tears at bay. Regroup, she told herself. Don't let him psych you out. She swallowed. "I know I didn't do my best work under Professor Clement. That's why I hoped to transfer to you. Do you think you could at least take a look at my proposal? I would really appreciate your feedback."

Professor Lawrence looked at the pendulum clock on the wall, rolled his eyes, and sighed. But he reached for the papers Jessica proffered. "Just the summary, I don't have time to read your entire proposal."

Jessica extracted the one-page summary and set it in the middle of the crocodile leather desk blotter. The Professor's lips turned down and his eyebrows drew together in the middle of his forehead. "Did you put any thought into this at all or did you just churn it out overnight in a misguided attempt to pander to my ego?"

With her teeth cutting into her lower lip and her nails pressing into her palms, Jessica managed to force tears to spill down her cheeks hoping if she could not impress him with her pandering to at least garner his sympathy. "Please, sir, if I don't get an R.A. position, I'm going to have to drop out of school. I'll probably end up working in some menial job for little better than minimum wage. I've invested three years of my life in this program. If I could continue without financial aid, believe me I would." Especially if that would have allowed me to stay with Professor Clement. He had never berated me or made me squirm.

Professor Lawrence removed his spectacles and wiped them with a cleaning tissue that he pulled out of his desk drawer. "Miss Richards, if you had anything to offer Chicago University as a scholar, I might find myself moved by your plight. But frankly, I can't see that your dropping out would present a great loss to the school."

Jessica pulled an embroidered handkerchief out of her pocket and dabbed at her eyes. It came away smeared with mascara and she hated to think what she looked like, but tears had always proved the most effective way to get what she needed. "Isn't there anything I can do to change your mind?"

Professor Lawrence studied Jessica from her Pucci pumps, long stocking-covered legs, and size-four Armani suit, pausing for a long while to stare at the cleavage revealed by the cut of the chenille jacket. He rubbed one finger under his lower lip. "I might make an exception in your case, however only if you can meet other criteria." He pushed back his shirt sleeve to examine his platinum Piguet watch. "I don't have time to discuss that option now, I've got another appointment starting in just a few minutes.." He pulled his leather-bound desk calendar closer and flipped through the pages. "I don't have office time available until the middle of next month."

Jessica sucked in her breath. She had no idea how she would cover her rent or pay her cell phone bill.

"Tell you what." Lawrence closed the calendar and looked up. The smile on his face raised the hairs on the back of Jessica's neck. "If you come over to my house this evening at eight-thirty I'll go over your options with you then." He scratched an address on a piece of paper and handed it to Jessica.

"Thank you, sir. I really appreciate your understanding." Rising to her feet, she tried to regain her composure. "I'll be there at eight-thirty." She stuffed her proposal back into the portfolio and stumbled to the door.

Outside of the building, the brisk air revived her somewhat. She pulled her cell from her pocket to turn the sound back on and noticed a missed call. Alyssa had tried to reach her again — one of half a dozen attempts in the past week. Busy with her research, Jessica had neither taken nor returned her calls. She didn't return this call either. Although Alyssa meant well, Jessica didn't need sympathy right now, she needed money. Once she got the R.A. position squared away, she and Alyssa could play catch up.

Jessica walked across campus and debated whether or not she should return to her apartment. The forty-five minute walk each way would eat up an hour and a half of the four hours she had to kill before making her appearance at Professor Lawrence's house. She headed for the Student Center instead. She could repair her makeup in the gymnasium locker room, check her e-mail at the Student Lounge, and send Alyssa a message to let her know that she might be out of touch for a few more days. That would leave her plenty of time to get something to eat and catch the bus that would take her up Sheridan Avenue to the Professor's house. Jessica had become all too familiar with the bus routes these past few weeks.

Chapter Four

When Jessica rang the bell next to the carved teak door, it opened although she couldn't see anyone inside. She stepped onto the Italian marble tile of the foyer to find a buxom blonde wearing a black lace garter belt, black stockings, six-inch stiletto heels, a steel chainlink necklace, and a leather dog collar around her neck, but nothing else. Jessica heard her portfolio and purse hit the tile, although she didn't remember letting go of them. She couldn't help staring at the blonde's creamy white skin unmarred by body hair while the woman pushed the door closed and turned the deadbolt. Her erect nipples stood out from pink areola centered on delectable D-cup breasts. Who are you? Why don't you have any clothes on? Jessica wanted to ask, but she couldn't get her mouth to cooperate.

"This way, Ms. Richards." The blonde turned on her heel and tapped her way across the tile down a wide, teak-paneled hallway lined with reproductions of Matisse, Dali, Kahlo, and O'Keeffe. At least Jessica assumed, once she got her feet to move so she could follow the blonde, that they were reproductions. Distracted by the undulating buttocks in front of her, she really couldn't give the pictures enough attention to determine how authentic they looked.

"In here." The woman opened a door and stepped aside.

Jessica started back toward the entrance. "My portfolio."

The woman grabbed her arm and guided her toward the doorway. "I'll get it for you."

Jessica stared at the hand on her bicep until the blonde gave her a nudge. She raised her chin and stepped into the darkened room. An antique, green-shaded banker's lamp on the large cherrywood desk provided the only illumination. The Professor sat in a leather armchair. He wore a leather vest, but no shirt, and his beady eyes peered out through a leather mask that covered the top half of his face. When Jessica stepped into the room, he closed the file folder on the desk in front of him.

She didn't know whether to laugh, scream, or run. Jessica forgot the Professor's ludicrous appearance when she saw another naked woman beside his desk. One of the most attractive women Jessica had ever seen, she knelt with her hands open, palms up on her stocking-clad thighs. Her red hair draped across her shoulders and partially covered small, pert breasts that Jessica wanted very much to touch.

The blonde had followed Jessica into the room and she mimicked the redhead's position on the opposite side of the Professor's desk. Both women gazed at the floor. The Professor ignored them, although Jessica wondered how he could think of anything else.

"I only take two kinds of students under advisement." The Professor stood, causing Jessica to tear her eyes away from the naked women in front of her. She gasped when she realized he wore no slacks, only leather chaps that left his genitals exposed and knee-high boots. "Excellent students and beautiful ones."

Jessica pressed her lips together to keep from laughing. *Who does this old fart think he is?* Her thoughts immediately turned somber, though. *What are these gorgeous women doing here?* His words sunk in. *Did he expect her to parade around naked for his entertainment?*

"Since you are only a mediocre student..." He paused to

let the word grate. Jessica hated having someone call her ordinary. She studied hard and put a lot of effort into her research. She just didn't take tests well. "... if you want to continue your studies at Chicago University you must take advantage of your beauty."

The Professor stepped around his desk and stood in front of Jessica. She recognized the spicy leather scent of John Varvatos Vintage, the cologne she had bought her father for Christmas. Now it made her nauseous. Professor Lawrence stroked her hair, then tangled the fingers of his left hand into the strands and yanked her head back.

Jessica tried to maintain her composure and avoid slapping the head of the Psychology Department. "Given that choice, I think I prefer to stay with Dr. Clement." She wondered if she could win enough from a sexual harassment suit to pay for the rest of her education. Jessica certainly had no intention of caving in like the two women on the floor.

"That's no longer an option, my dear." Without releasing her hair, Professor Lawrence drew one finger of his right hand along her jaw line, down her neck, and in between her breasts.

She tried to jerk away, but his grip on her hair tightened and she found herself fighting an urge to turn her head and bite his finger. If she assaulted him, she would have less of a case, she reminded herself.

"Now, your options are to give yourself to me as my slave or leave the University. If you defy me, I will prevent you from getting your thesis approved and block any research proposal you put in front of the faculty."

Jessica scoffed. "You can't do this, it's harassment."

"And what proof do you have of that?" Professor Lawrence reached inside her bra cup and pinched Jessica's nipple until she gasped. With his hand gripping her hair, she couldn't escape his groping without hurting him, which wouldn't help her university career. "These women serve me willingly. They will deny any allegations you make about this conversation. And I can easily reject your work based on its merit, or should I say lack thereof.

"Instead, I'm offering you an opportunity to continue your education with my backing. If you choose not to take advantage of it, you must accept the consequences."

Jessica took a long, slow breath. Given the choice between sacrificing the time she had invested in graduate school and putting up with the Professor's little power games, she was tempted to choose the latter. She could prance around naked as easily as the two women at her feet. They didn't seem to have suffered any ill effects, although she supposed if the Professor forced them to have sex with him it wouldn't show in their demeanor.

Professor Lawrence tugged her hair and pulled her into a polished oak armchair. Without releasing her hair, he snapped his fingers. The two naked women pulled nylon cord from one of the drawers in the cherrywood file cabinet next to the Professor's desk. Jessica debated, for a moment, whether nor not she should resist. She tried to remember what her texts had said about bondage deviants. While she hesitated, the women tied Jessica's wrists and ankles to the arms and legs of the chair. For the first time in her life, she felt helpless and she did not like the sensation.

"I'm going to leave you here to contemplate your options." Professor Lawrence released her hair so suddenly, Jessica's chin dropped to her chest. "You must choose between becoming my slave or abandoning your academic prospects at this university." He stepped behind her, lowered his face to ear, and grabbed a breast in each hand. "I beat my slaves regularly. I use them sexually and allow any of my colleagues willing to pay for the privilege to use them as well. I do not permit them to wear clothing in my home, including when I entertain."

Jessica's eyes widened at his words and the moisture

disappeared from her mouth. She could feel her heart pounding in her chest and found it difficult to draw air into her lungs.

He took her earlobe in his teeth and bit it until she cried out in pain. "But all my slaves get excellent publishing credits and references. They succeed whether they choose academia or private practice. My reputation in the field jumpstarts their careers."

He stood upright. "Of course, if you leave the University you'll have forfeited all the work that you have done to date. Not only will you have to start over, you will have to do so with the disgrace of rejection from this institution hanging over you."

Jessica could hear the door opening behind her. "Consider all the consequences before you make your choice."

The naked blonde pulled the chain to turn out the light and followed him and the redhead out of the office. The door closed behind them leaving Jessica in darkness. She tried to reassure herself that the Professor didn't seriously think he could beat her and pimp her out to other faculty members. Geez, he's full of himself. She pushed her shoulders back against the chair. Certainly none of the other faculty members would participate in his sick games.

Worst case scenario, she'd have to prance around naked and let him spank her a couple of times. Compared to getting kicked out of the University and starting over somewhere else — assuming she could find another college to admit her — that didn't seem so bad. And he couldn't possibly expect her to have sex with him. She closed her eyes. What if he did? Right now she had no financial recourse. In nine days she would have no place to live. She couldn't even sleep in her car, since she no longer had one. She had no income, no employable skills, and no one who would take her in.

Accepting his offer seemed no better than joining the hookers parading up and down Rush Street. On the other hand, Lawrence had former students and colleagues at every school in the country. Prostituting herself to him at least allowed her to maintain her reputation and respectability. If she didn't give him what he wanted, he had the ability to squash her career before it started. If she did, he could ease her transition from student to professional.

She could pretend to serve him, so he would approve her thesis and get her dissertation proposal through the faculty panel. As an R.A., she could get paid to do the research she needed to complete her work. His assistants had their findings published in the most prestigious journals. Jessica took a deep breath and squirmed against the bindings around her wrists and ankles. Although she had planned to use the full eight years allotted to finish her doctoral work, she knew of students who had completed their dissertation in two. Could she stomach what he asked of her for that long?

Chapter Five

Jessica heard the door open and a switch flip. Light from a brass ceiling fixture bathed the room. She gripped the arms of the chair for a moment, then relaxed her fingers. She didn't want the Professor to see her fear or trepidation. Pressing her lips together, she tried to keep her breathing steady.

"Your decision?" Lawrence stepped around her chair and leaned his ample rear on the corner of his desk.

"If I serve you," Jessica worked to keep her voice from quavering, pressing her fingers against the arms of her chair rather than wrapping her hands around them. "I get a paid R.A. position and my dissertation proposal gets approved?" She tried to appear calm and collected despite feeling anything but.

He smiled. "Yes, dear, but you still have to do the work. I will facilitate approval of your research topic and your dissertation defense, but you must do the required research and write the document." He snapped his fingers and the two naked women knelt beside her chair and untied the ropes.

Jessica slid from the chair to her knees.

"Strip."

She unbuttoned her jacket top and slipped it off her shoulders, folding it and setting it on the chair. Exposed to Lawrence's leering grin, she unzipped her skirt rather than remove the only fabric now covering her chest. Unable to remove the narrow skirt while kneeling, afraid to rise, Jessica reached behind her back to unfasten her brassiere. She hesitated before letting the satin cups fall free from her breasts. The idea of exposing herself to this dirty old man caused bile to rise to her throat.

"You may stand to remove the rest of your clothing."

Jessica pulled herself to her feet, using the arm of the chair, trying to regain her composure. She slid the skirt down her hips, stepped out of it, folded it neatly and added it to the pile on the seat.

"You will never wear pantyhose again. Buy yourself a garter belt and some real stockings."

"Yes, sir," Jessica pulled the pantyhose and her silk thong down her legs.

"That's 'Yes, Master.' "

"Yes, Master." Jessica returned to her knees. The other women buckled leather cuffs around her wrists and ankles. She resisted an urge to twist them around so they didn't press into her skin.

Stepping close again, Lawrence clasped a leather collar around Jessica's neck. Even though it didn't fit as tightly as the cuffs, Jessica found breathing difficult as if her world collapsing around her reduced the available air and the collar kept what was left from getting to her lungs.

Lawrence clipped a leash to the front ring of the collar and dragged Jessica out of the room. Despite her attempts to walk with pride and not let him browbeat her, Jessica found herself stumbling after the Professor. At the end of the hall, he stepped to one side and pushed her toward a door that opened on a dimly lit staircase and handed the leash to the blonde, stating: "Get her ready, Felicia."

The blonde led Jessica down the narrow, wooden stairs and she felt a draft as they neared the bottom. She followed Felicia into a cavernous room, the cement floor cold against her bare feet. Several X-shaped crosses of polished oak lined one wall. Half a dozen cages were scattered about the room along with padded tables and benches in unfamiliar configurations. Jessica suppressed a snicker — the room looked like something off an S&M porn site — until she saw the collection of whips that hung from a rack in the center of the room. Wooden and metal paddles, handcuffs, and bundles of rope filled an open shelving unit. A tall oak cabinet stood against the far wall.

The blonde continued through the room. She opened a door to a large bathroom, reached in to flip on the light, and stepped aside. "You need to wash the makeup off your face and use the toilet. It will be your last chance to do so for a while."

Jessica stepped past Felicia's amazing breasts. She reached for the knob to close the door behind herself, but the blonde kept her hand on it. "We aren't permitted to close doors, ever."

Jessica grimaced and stepped to the marble sink.

"There's remover in the cabinet," Felicia said.

Jessica pulled the mirror aside, took out the eye makeup remover and a couple of cotton squares and went to work. She washed her face, blotted it dry, and looked at the blonde, who turned her eyes toward the toilet. Reluctantly, Jessica lifted the lid, turned, and sat down. Even when she had to take witnessed drug tests at school, they allowed her the privacy of a stall. Getting her body to cooperate under scrutiny seemed to take forever. When she finally rose, she felt the heat of embarrassment on her cheeks. Looking in the mirror while washing her hands, she saw the redness extended down her long neck.

She flipped off the light and emerged from the bathroom. Felicia took Jessica's leash, led her over to one of the crosses where the redhead stood waiting, and guided Jessica to a position standing with her face between the two upper arms of the cross. The polished wood felt cold against her naked skin. The redhead knelt down and clipped Jessica's ankle cuffs to eyebolts while Felicia lifted first one arm and then the other, hooking the leather cuffs to the cross. Jessica heard boot heels on the concrete floor and listened while they paused in the center of the room. She trembled, no longer able to pretend she had no fear.

The spicy leather scent of Vintage enveloped her and a rough hand caressed her. Her trembling made her knees buckle and she hung from her wrists until she regained her footing. The Professor muttered something unintelligible under his breath. Jessica heard the lash before she felt it: it whistled through the air then sliced across her flesh. She cried out, startled by the pain that reverberated through her. Before she could fully process the torment, another stroke and then another landed across her rear. The lash moved up her back, cutting into her shoulders, wrapping around to sting her breasts. Jessica screamed. "Please," she begged. "Please stop, I'll do whatever you say, please." The man is a lunatic. What makes him think he can get away with this?

The whip stopped, but something else pummeled her shoulders. Long leather strips struck her back in unison, biting the already tender flesh. "No more, please." She sobbed, her body shaking, she hung from her wrists again and they ached from supporting her weight. The lashes flayed her back, her rear, her legs. How had she ended up in this predicament? Why had her father deserted her? Why hadn't Louis Foster saved her inheritance?

The whistling and slapping of the leather stopped. "Felicia, you can take over. Sandra, come with me." The boot heels marched across the cement floor and fingernails dragged across the welts on Jessica's back. But much to her relief, someone unclipped her wrists and her ankles and a shoulder under her arm guided Jessica over to one of the padded tables. Blonde hair came into focus through Jessica's tears. Felicia made Jessica sit on the table, but the leather pressed into her flayed flesh.

"No, please," Jessica whispered.

Felicia pushed her flat on the table and pulled her hands above her head. Before Jessica could get her wits about her, she found herself attached to the table by wrists and ankles. She struggled, but her own weight pressed her bruised skin into the leather padding. It hurt less if she didn't fight. She had never hurt this much, or felt so helpless, in her entire life. She couldn't believe she had agreed to let the Professor subject her to this.

Wheels squeaked and Felicia rolled a set of plastic drawers up alongside the table. She opened the top drawer, bent over it for a moment and stood upright to stare down at Jessica. The wicked glint in Felicia's eyes sent a chill down Jessica's back. The blonde reached out with one hand, caressed Jessica's cheek, and ran a finger across her lips and down her neck. Felicia took the white mound of Jessica's right breast in her hand and leaned over to take the nipple in her mouth. Felicia bit down hard and Jessica shrieked. Felicia pulled her mouth away, fastened a metal clamp to Jessica's nipple and tightened it until Jessica shrieked again. Then Felicia bit and clamped Jessica's left breast. Jessica wondered how much pain she would have to endure before she passed out.

Felicia reached into the drawer again and brought out a giant red dildo. She showed it to Jessica and brought it to her mouth. "Kiss it."

Jessica turned her head away in disgust. Felicia grabbed her hair and pulled her face back to the dildo. "I said kiss it." She shoved the dildo between Jessica's lips causing her to gag and choke. "That's better." Felicia pulled the dildo away and dragged it between Jessica's breasts, down her stomach, and between her legs.

"No, please," Jessica whispered, knowing Felicia would ignore her plea.

Felicia shoved the dildo into Jessica and laughed at the pained moan that emerged from Jessica's lips. She felt as if it had ripped her insides open and left her even more vulnerable and violated.

"You can beg all you want, Jessica. You're mine for the rest of the night. I have Master's permission to do anything to you that I want." Felicia pulled the dildo partially out and rammed it back in, hitting Jessica's cervix and sending another stabbing pain to join the others permeating her body. Then, Felicia pulled a second, slightly smaller dildo from the drawer. She made Jessica lick it and suck on it until it was slick with saliva. Jessica watched wide-eyed as Felicia, never taking her blue eyes away from Jessica's, moved the dildo between Jessica's legs. When it pressed against her rectum, Jessica clenched her cheeks.

"This is going inside you, no matter what you do. If you don't relax and stop resisting it's going to hurt a lot more."

Jessica closed her eyes, hot tears seeping out between her lashes. She pressed her lips together and tried to relax, but her sphincter muscles only tightened more. Felicia pushed the second dildo inside her and Jessica screamed as the rigid plastic shredded her insides and tore her apart. Each time she thought she had endured the ultimate in pain and humiliation, her tormentors created new ways to torture her. Jessica didn't think she could survive. She wasn't sure she wanted to.

Felicia leaned over and kissed Jessica on the lips.

Jessica found her head lifting off the table almost without her wishing it. Her lips clung to Felicia's, desperate for any touch that didn't bring pain, any contact that comforted. Felicia chuckled and put one hand on either side of Jessica's head, tangling her fingers in long black hair. She pressed her lips to Jessica's and teased them with her tongue. Jessica whimpered and did not resist Felicia's tongue, tasting of chocolate and mint, probing her mouth. Then Felicia bit

Jessica's lower lip until she cried out. Jessica could feel the lip swelling, but Felicia's betrayal caused Jessica more pain than her lip.

She heard Felicia rummaging about in the drawer again, but Jessica didn't bother to open her eyes even when she felt pinch after pinch on her labia. She lost count of the clamps — none of them hurt as much as her nipples — and drifted away from the agony. Then, Felicia closed a clamp on her clit and Jessica screamed again, the excruciating pain jerking her back to the table and the woman standing beside it.

Jessica smelled phosphorous and opened her eyes to see Felicia holding a black candle over Jessica's stomach. The flame make the blonde's eyes glitter. Her grin got bigger, revealing white teeth against pink lips, and she tipped the candle. The hot wax spilled onto Jessica's abdomen, eliciting a screech. She wept, wishing she could die, cursing the self indulgence and stupidity that had gotten her into this predicament.

Felicia continued to burn the candle, tipping it when the melting wax accumulated, coating Jessica's breasts, belly, and inner thighs with wax. Jessica longed to pass out to escape this hellish nightmare. One pain faded into another and she could no longer distinguish specific areas — everything throbbed in agony, inside and out.

When the candle had shrunk to an inch, Felicity stuck the nub in Jessica's navel and watched it burn itself out. Jessica didn't have breath enough to scream, the agony sucking the air from her lungs. Before she could recover, a new pain penetrated her anguish. She looked down to see Felicia swinging a riding crop at the bottom of her feet. Each blow's sting added to the avalanche of torment.

When Felicia had covered the soles of Jessica's feet with welts, a different voice penetrated the fog of pain clouding her mind. "Master wants you to fix him breakfast, then you can go to bed. I'll take over here." Jessica finally realized the voice belonged to Sandra. Would the beautiful redhead who Jessica yearned to caress prove as cruel as Felicia?

Sandra wiped hair away from Jessica's eyes and lifted her head with one arm under her shoulders. "Here, have some water." The redhead held a metal cup to Jessica's lips and let a little liquid trickle down her throat. Jessica wanted to gulp from the cup to ease her parched mouth, but Sandra only let her have a few sips then lowered her head to the table and kissed her brow. Jessica closed her eyes, hoping she could sleep now.

Stabbing pain jerked her back to alertness as Sandra removed one of the nipple clamps allowing blood to flow back into tissue that had become numb. Sandra pulled off the other nipple clamp and then removed the ones that lined Jessica's labia. Each time shooting pain ripped away the numbness that had settled in since Felicia had put on the clamps. Jessica feared the clamps had ripped open her flesh.

Jessica didn't have the stamina left to scream. She tried to find her equilibrium. Before she could recover from the onslaught to her nerve endings, cold penetrated the pain in her breasts. Sandra had a hunk of ice in her hand and rubbed it across any of Jessica's skin not covered by candle wax. Jessica sucked in her breath, but couldn't get enough air into her lungs. Panting, gasping for air, Jessica no longer tried giving voice to her pleas for the torment to stop. She knew no one would listen.

In a daze she wondered if anyone would notice her disappearance. But, since Louis Foster broke his news, she had ignored most phone calls and messages. While Jessica immersed herself in her research, only Alyssa had kept trying to reach her. By now, even she would have given up.

Melted ice and sweat pooled up on the leather beside Jessica. Sandra held a stainless steel rod in front of Jessica's eyes. On one end a couple dozen sharp pins protruded from a spinning wheel. Jessica recognized the device Dr.

Wartenberg had invented to test nerve reactions. Sandra ran it across Jessica's breasts, sides, legs, feet, and labia, pricking her tender skin. Jessica groaned, but couldn't even flinch away from the pain. Sandra unclipped Jessica's ankles and lifted her feet, exposing her raw behind. The Wartenberg wheel pricked the welts, renewing the agony that had dissipated in the face of that inflicted elsewhere on her body.

Chapter Six

Jessica gave up trying to keep track of who abused her when and how — pain blurred her vision so she could no longer distinguish Sandra's red hair from Felicia's blonde locks. She only knew the Professor wielded the instruments torturing her when the scent of Vintage penetrated the haze enveloping Jessica's mind. She couldn't remember the last time she had eaten or slept. Only the skin on her face didn't hurt — every other inch of her hide pulsed and throbbed. Welts, burns, pricks, bruises, and blisters covered her body. The dildos inside her stretched her tender membranes. Tears no longer filled her eyes, her mouth was parched and dry.

She hung from the ceiling, suspended by rope binding her breasts and cutting into her crotch, with her wrists tied behind her back and her ankles tied to her thighs. Hands pushed her back and forth and metal poked at her welts. Her greasy hair hung down over her face and her own odor offended her.

"Who are you?" She heard the Professor's voice over the creaking of the rope.

"Your slave, Master." Jessica forced the words through cracked lips. Obedience offered her the only hope of ending the torment.

"What can I do to you?"

"Anything you wish, Master." He had proven that already.

A pulley squeaked and the cement floor came up to meet

Jessica's face. The cold felt good against the heat of her pain. Someone removed the ropes and moved her limbs until circulation returned. This time the metal cup stayed against her lips until she had drunk her fill.

"Get her cleaned up." The spice and leather scent faded away.

Could the torment have stopped? Or did they just intend to prepare her for some new torture? Supported on either side by Felicia and Sandra, Jessica stumbled into the bathroom. The two women sat her on the toilet, then helped her into the shower. One of the women stepped into the stall and Jessica leaned against the wall while her hair was shampooed and rinsed. Soft, soapy hands slid gently across her raw skin. The warm water smarted everywhere it touched, but it washed away the stinging salt from her sweat. The fruity scent of the soap and shampoo erased the musky odor that made her nauseous. Clean never felt so good and hurt so much at the same time.

Even the soft terrycloth towel burned as it patted her tender skin. A fleece blanket was wrapped around her and Sandra led Jessica out of the bathroom to one of the cages. Once inside, she heard a lock click. She curled up in the corner. Too exhausted to contemplate the hole she seemed to have dropped into, she fell asleep. She woke when a cane poked at her and she found the cage door open. Jessica crawled out of the cage, leaving the blanket behind, and knelt on the floor. Desperate to avoid any more pain, she tried to mimic the position she had seen Sandra and Felicia take in the Master's office: rear on her heels, hands on her thighs, palms up, back straight, knees open, eyes down.

The Professor stepped in front of her, one foot on either side of her left thigh, his crotch in her face. She grimaced, but kissed his limp penis, not sure if by doing so she consented to prostitution or became a rape victim. Although his penis twitched slightly at the touch of her lips, it didn't get any bigger or more erect. Jessica wasn't sure how he wanted her to proceed. The Professor grabbed the back of her head and pressed her face into his groin, so she licked his length and took the head into her mouth. Still no reaction. Sucking the tip, she pulled the entire length between her lips and ran her tongue up and down it. Although it didn't respond, the Professor put a hand on either side of her head, lacing his fingers in her still damp hair.

Jessica had only three lovers, all her own age. She had never touched a man who didn't respond to her caresses and didn't know what to do now. The Professor kept her face tight in his crotch and moaned with what she hoped was pleasure, so she kept trying. She licked, sucked, and stroked using her lips, her tongue, her fingers. His penis never reacted, but the Professor tightened his grip on her hair and pushed her face harder against him. He thrust his hips forward, and to her surprise a dribble of acrid ejaculate trickled into her mouth. Instinctively, Jessica swallowed.

The Professor pulled back. "Good, girl." He patted her on the head.

He walked away and Sandra handed her an energy bar and a cup of water. Jessica unwrapped the bar and bit into it, grateful to chase away the Professor's foul taste. Even though dry and bland, the peanut flavor was fabulous. Jessica licked the crumbs from the wrapper and emptied the cup. Sandra pointed to the cage and Jessica crawled back inside and wrapped herself in the blanket. She had no idea a man could come without ever getting hard. At least if the Professor was impotent, she could hope that he wouldn't require any additional sexual services. As repulsive as she found taking him in her mouth, the idea of him mounting her made her stomach churn.

Too tired to think of much beyond the temporary reprieve from additional pain, Jessica closed her eyes. This time, she slept until she woke on her own in the empty dungeon.

She tried to calculate how long since she had stripped off her clothes and descended into hell. But without a watch or clock or even a window to the world outside, she had no reference to judge the passage of time. She realized it didn't really matter. The man who called himself her Master would know how much time she had spent in the dungeon and she would have to wait until he decided to allow her to emerge.

Chapter Seven

Sandra opened the cage and walked over to one of the padded tables. Jessica cringed, afraid to imagine what the redhead planned to do to her now. Worried that defiance would only bring more pain, she crawled out of the cage and up onto the table. She lay down on her back, slowly to avoid aggravating the welts.

"Turn over." Sandra opened a blue bottle and Jessica smelled marigolds and witch hazel.

Jessica eased herself around so she lay on her stomach, her sore and bruised breasts protesting when she let the weight of her chest rest on them. Sandra squeezed out lotion from the bottle onto Jessica's skin and she shivered at the cold. Although she winced at the pressure of Sandra's palms spreading the lotion across her back and buttocks, it felt good against her bruised skin.

"May I ask what that is?"

"Arnica, also known as Leopard's Bane. It will help your bruises heal faster. I'll give you this bottle to take home. You need to keep a supply on hand. You'll be expected to use it whenever you're beaten to make sure you heal as quickly as possible so you can be beaten again."

"Yes, Ma'am. Thank you." Home. That one word offered enough hope of refuge and escape, at least temporarily, from hell, that Jessica ignored Sandra's explanation of why she would need to stock up on arnica.

Sandra led Jessica, clutching the bottle of arnica, up the stairs to the Professor's office. When they entered, Sandra knelt on the plush carpet on one side of the desk and Jessica mimicked her position on the other. The Professor sat at in his chair, occasionally turning pages in the folder in front of him. Jessica's clothing still lay folded on the leather wingback where she had left it, her Lauren Merkin handbag on top of the pile.

Jessica sensed rather than saw the Professor remove his glasses and clean them. Then he rose and stepped in front of her, a length of quarter-inch chain links in one hand and a pair of pliers in the other. He draped the links across her neck, the metal cold against her skin, and joined them with a partially opened one. Then he used the pliers to close the last link. She looked at the necklace around Sandra's neck and realized she now wore an identical one.

"This collar signifies my ownership of you. You cannot remove it. You will wear the dog collar whenever you serve. But the chains will stay around your neck forever."

Forever. NO! Jessica screamed in her mind. Aloud, she said: "Yes, Master. Thank you, Master." But she promised herself she would not wear the collar a minute longer than necessary to get her doctorate.

"You must always make yourself available to meet my needs. I expect you to keep yourself shaved of all body hair, appropriately groomed, and dressed. You will never wear slacks, only dresses and skirts — and no pantyhose. You may wear a bra, but never panties. You should never wear less than a three-inch heel and when you come here to serve, you will wear stilettos. You will always remove your clothing and hang it in the front closet before you join me. Do you understand?"

Jessica reeled as the Professor heaped more indignities on her already battered psyche. But she only said: "Yes, Master. Thank you, Master."

"You may get dressed now."

"Yes, Master. Thank you, Master." Jessica rose to her feet and put on her bra, skirt and jacket top. She stuffed her lace panties and silk hose in one pocket and the bottle of arnica in the other and slipped her naked feet into her pumps.

The Professor smiled and handed Jessica her embossed Bosca leather portfolio. "I have noted the problems in your dissertation proposal. You need to address them and have this ready for me to present to the panel next week."

"Yes, Master. Thank you, Master."

"Felicia will drive you home now. I'll let you know when I want you back here."

"Yes, Master. Thank you, Master."

Jessica clutched her portfolio and her purse to her chest and stumbled out into the hallway. Felicia, wearing a black gabardine trench coat waited by the front door and Jessica followed her to a red Mazda Miata parked in the driveway. Jessica's instructions on which way to turn were the only words they exchanged during the twenty-minute drive.

Inside her apartment, Jessica dropped to her knees on the blue Persian carpet in front of her sofa, put her face in her hands and wept. Her shoulders shook with her sobs. Unable to stop crying, or shaking she extracted her cell phone from her purse. The battery had died. When she plugged it into the charger and turned it on, she stared at the date. Four days had elapsed since she had ventured to Professor Lawrence's office in search of a new advisor. She had missed six calls, five from Alyssa and one from a number she didn't recognize. Alyssa had left two voice mails, both expressing concern and begging Jessica to call.

Jessica used her desk chair to pull herself to her feet, tottered into the bathroom, and splashed cold water on her face until she could stop crying and breathe normally. Get a grip, she told herself. She avoided looking in the mirror and flipped off the light. Her hands shaking, she stripped off her clothing, crawled into bed, and pulled the blankets over her head. She cried herself to sleep.

J

The next morning, Jessica finally forced herself to climb out of bed and boot up her computer. Sitting on an ice bag, eating granola cereal straight out of the box, she stared at the screen without seeing it, trying to focus long enough to deal with her e-mail. Once she had deleted the spam from her inbox, Jessica had six e-mails from Alyssa. One from the University confirmed her acceptance as a Research Assistant under Professor Lawrence and listed detailed expectations, requirements, and salary. When she saw how little her prostitution was worth, Jessica wailed. She would have done better walking the streets. More tears trickled down her cheeks. She needed to prevent another bout of hysteria and move on. Street-walking might pay better, but one arrest and she could kiss her psychology career goodbye.

Pushing away the thought of how low she had sunk, she responded to one of Alyssa's e-mails. "Sorry, I've been out of touch. Nothing personal, just regrouping, trying to make sure I have enough money to finish my doctorate. I've managed to secure a research position with the head of the psych department. Very prestigious. Should help a lot when I go job searching. Unfortunately, between that and my own research, I'm not going to have much in the way of free time." Jessica reread the message three times to assure herself that none of her desperation, pain, and humiliation had seeped through, trying to find reassurance in the reality painted by her words.

Stepping around the portfolio on the floor where she had dropped it, unwilling to face any vestige of the Professor, even his handwriting, Jessica wandered into the kitchen. She searched her refrigerator for something else edible. After tossing rotten produce, expired milk, and moldy Prosciutto into the garbage, she extracted a small wedge of brie. She ate it standing up with Courtney's cracked pepper water crackers from the box and washed it down with a third of a bottle of Cullen's chardonnay.

Feeling a little steadier on her feet, Jessica went to the bathroom. Washing up afterwards, she allowed her eyes to focus on the face in the mirror. She had dark circles under her eyes, her lips still showed signs of cracked dryness, and her green eyes had a pained, haunted look. But what horrified her most were the links around her neck and all they represented. The cheese transformed into a rock in her stomach as recognition pierced the fog surrounding her brain. She remembered seeing a choker of links around Alyssa's husband's neck. She had never thought him the type to wear jewelry and stainless steel rather than gold seemed a strange choice. Although he wore a different design, Jessica now had to wonder if his necklace had more meaning than she had ever suspected.

Jessica put one hand over her mouth, suppressing a shriek that would have sent her neighbors rushing to call the police. She returned to her computer and spent the next four hours learning more than she cared to know about people who lived as slaves to Masters and Mistresses. Her head aching, her welts and bruises throbbing, she shut down the computer and crawled back into bed even though it was only noon.

J

The next morning, Jessica finally picked the portfolio off the floor and flipped through Professor Lawrence's notes on her dissertation proposal while she sipped her coffee and nibbled a croissant she had found in the freezer and heated in the microwave. She really couldn't argue with any of his suggestions. And some of his changes would make the research easier.

Three days later she had completed the revised proposal. As the bottle instructed, she had applied the arnica twice daily and most of her bruises had faded to a mild discoloration. She could no longer feel any welts with her hand. Her pantry and freezer empty, she decided to venture out to the grocery store. She reached for her jeans, hesitated and grabbed a skirt and blouse instead. Digging in her lingerie drawer, she found a black lace garter belt she had worn to a birthday celebration for one of her boyfriends and a pair of intact stockings. She put the revised proposal in an envelope and addressed it to the Professor's office at the University.

After stopping at the post office to buy stamps, she visited Marshall Field's to pick up several more pairs of stockings and another garter belt. She passed by the Whole Foods, opting instead for the less expensive Jewel. Although she now had an income, she still would earn barely enough to cover her living expenses. With a basket filled mostly with sale items, Jessica checked out and headed back to her apartment. Her cell rang just after she set the bags on the tile kitchen counter.

She stared at the display. How could she face Alyssa after what she had done? But the daily e-mails from her friend had gotten more and more insistent — Alyssa apparently wouldn't take Jessica's written word that she was okay. Jessica hit the send button just before the call went to voice mail.

"You poor dear, you have to let me help you."

"Really, Alyssa, I'm okay. The R.A. position will cover my living expenses. I'll just have to adjust my financial priorities."

"I know that's going to be difficult for you. At least let me take you out to lunch."

Jessica put her hand to the collar around her neck. "Thanks, hon, but I'm pretty busy right now putting my proposal together. Then I've got to get started on my research. Under the circumstances, I'm going to try to accelerate things and finish in two years."

"I bet you haven't been out to lunch since your father died, have you? I'll treat you to McCormick & Schmick's in the Loop."

Jessica closed her eyes. The memory of seared yellowfin with wasabi made her mouth water. She walked into her bedroom and pulled open the doors to her closet. She usually wore her black turtleneck with jeans, but she could put it on over a skirt. "You sure know how to tempt a girl."

"Tomorrow at eleven-thirty?"

Chapter Eight

Jessica cringed as she pulled nylon stockings over freshly shaved legs, but she couldn't justify paying three times as much for silk. She had nicked herself twice shaving her labia, but now that the bruises and welts from her four days in the Professor's dungeon had healed, she dared not put that task off any longer. She didn't know how often he would demand her presence, but didn't want to risk getting called to report immediately and not having time to shave. Although she had contemplated visiting a salon for a wax job, she could no longer afford to spend a hundred and twenty dollars, plus another eighty for her pubic hair, every week. She would just have to become more adept with a razor.

Alyssa waited for her outside the restaurant. Seeing the short, heavy-set woman with mousy brown hair, dark brown eyes, and ruddy complexion for the first time since the funeral, Jessica realized how, in many ways, Alyssa had taken on her mother's role. Twenty-six years apart, she knew they didn't seem to have much in common. But, Alyssa had stood by Jessica while she buried both parents and always had an ear or a shoulder available for her.

Although she usually preferred jeans and men's shirts, today Alyssa had chosen black slacks and a simple black sweater which she wore under her leather coat. As usual, she wore no makeup, nail polish, or perfume.

"How did you get here, dear." Alyssa wrapped her arms

around Jessica's waist then stood on tiptoe to kiss her on the cheek.

"Bus."

"Is your car in the shop?"

"I had to sell it — couldn't afford the payments or the insurance." Jessica pulled open the heavy glass door and let Alyssa step inside in front of her.

The aromas of freshly baked bread, garlic, and cooking olive oil wafted towards them as they approached the host stand. When they had taken their seats in the dark wooden booths, Alyssa reached over and patted Jessica's hand. "We're going to forget all about your troubles today, dear, and splurge on a truly extravagant lunch. Appetizers, dessert, wine ..."

At that moment, the waiter stepped in front of their table. "Can I get you ladies something to drink."

Alyssa reached for the wine list and studied it only for a moment. "We'll take a bottle of the New Zealand Sauvignon blanc."

"Yes, Ma'am." The waiter turned on his heel.

Alyssa smiled. "Since you're not driving, you can indulge. I'll give you a ride home so you don't even have to take the bus."

Jessica studied the menu rather than give in to her urge to confess all the details of the last week and a half to Alyssa. The collar felt heavy under her turtleneck, and she couldn't help but think of the one around Klark's neck. He and Alyssa had stayed together for almost twenty years, although Jessica now had to reevaluate her opinion of their relationship. She set the menu down and shared only the particulars of her father's ruin, the adjustments she had made in her financial commitments, and the details of the research she would start as soon as she had Professor Lawrence's approval.

"Anxiety disorder?" Alyssa inhaled the aroma of the wine sample poured by the waiter and took a sip. "I thought you wanted to study depression?" She nodded to the waiter who filled her glass and Jessica's.

"I would have preferred that, yes." Jessica tasted her wine and enjoyed the buttery vanilla flavor and the lemon-grass aroma. "But, I need a paid position to continue and Professor Clement doesn't have an opening for an R.A."

Alyssa twirled her wine glass by the stem. "This Professor Lawrence, his first name is William?"

Jessica nodded.

Alyssa pressed her lips together. "He doesn't have the best reputation."

"Within the field he does."

The waiter took their order and Jessica tried to change the subject. "How is Klark?"

Alyssa smiled. "Wonderful. But that's another subject." She raised one eyebrow above the other. "Are you sure this professor is your only option?"

Jessica nodded. "Everyone who's studied under him has gone on to stellar careers. With him as a mentor, I'll have more options and better opportunities."

"Just remember, dear. You can always confide in me. Nothing you could encounter would shock me and I want you to understand that you can tell me absolutely anything." Alyssa took a sip of her wine. "And, I could offer you advice on more subjects than you might realize from our prior conversations."

Jessica tilted her head to one side and wondered what Alyssa knew about the Professor. Although tempted to ask, her reticence about sharing what she had allowed herself to suffer, stopped her. The arrival of their appetizers provided the perfect segue. "Thanks so much for dragging me out to lunch. You can't imagine how much I appreciate it. I'm reduced to eating domestic cheese and cooking for myself." Jessica took a bite of the seared, yellowfin tuna and let the morsel melt in her mouth savoring the rich flavor and firm texture. "Oh, this is exquisite." She let the flavors chase away memories of the torment she had suffered and smiled.

Alyssa dipped a piece of fried calamari in a yellow sauce and smiled back. "I'm glad you're enjoying it, dear. I think I shall have to make it a habit of indulging you frequently so you don't suffer too much in your new circumstances."

"You can't afford that." Alyssa had returned to school to study art a year ago, after dropping out when she was Jessica's age. She hadn't held a job, that Jessica knew of, in all that time.

"Don't tell me what I can afford." Alyssa raised an eyebrow again. "We're not rich, but Klark earns a nice income. I can take my friends out to lunch occasionally if I choose."

Jessica reached for the sourdough bread to distract herself from the tears gathering in her eyes. "You're so sweet. You don't know how much I really needed this."

After indulging in the tuna appetizer and the pan fried oysters, Jessica didn't have room for dessert. Alyssa insisted that she order the chocolate truffle cake to go and take it home with the half-full bottle of wine. When she dropped Jessica off in front of her apartment building, Alyssa repeated her earlier statement. "Remember, you can always confide in me. Don't hesitate to call if you need someone to talk to who you can tell anything, absolutely anything."

Jessica nestled her head against Alyssa's shoulder and enjoyed the woman's arms wrapped around her. But she pulled away without sharing any of the thoughts or questions running rampant through her mind. "Thanks for everything. I truly enjoyed this afternoon."

J

Summoned to the Professor's home the following Monday, Jessica paused on the front steps before ringing the bell. Her knees threatened to buckle at the thought of what waited for her inside the house. She closed her eyes tight and pressed her lips together, trying to keep the tears at bay. Finally, with a shaking hand, she reached for the lighted button in the brass plate next to the teak door.

Sandra admitted her, waited while Jessica hung her clothing in the front closet. She buckled a dog collar around her neck, then led her up the wide teak staircase with polished ebony bannister. Like her, Sandra wore only hose, garter belts, and her collars. They found the Professor in his bedroom naked, lying face down on a padded leather massage table.

A king-size bed with curved cherrywood head and footboards filled a third of the room. A silver shield with a gold double-tailed lion across the top on a red background and a red cross with indentations hung over the marble fireplace with crossed swords displayed behind it. Cherrywood bureaus stood against the walls on either side of the fireplace which had a fake log engulfed in gas-fed flames.

Sandra handed Jessica a bottle of sandalwood-scented massage oil and left the room. Jessica poured oil into her hands, rubbed them together to warm it, and massaged it into the Professor's skin. The hair on his back was rough against her palms and her fingers weren't strong enough to manipulate through the rolls of fat to get to his muscles. But she concentrated on delivering the most sensual massage she had ever given, using her hands and forearms to stroke his skin and rub the oil in. If she pleased him, perhaps she could hope he would forgo beating her this afternoon.

He seemed content with her ministrations, and when he rolled over onto his back she rubbed oil into his chest and arms, allowing her breasts to touch him as she reached across him. He grabbed her hair and guided her head toward his crotch. Bile rose to her throat, but she knew what he expected of her and leaned down to take him in her mouth. Again he came without ever getting hard and Jessica swallowed the bitter fluid.

"I'm having a party Friday night for like-minded faculty. Sandra will explain what's expected of you before you leave."

"Yes, Master. Thank you, Master." Jessica waited a few minutes, but since he didn't say anything else, she assumed he expected her to leave. She wanted very much to ask him about her dissertation proposal, but guessed he needed to be the one to bring it up. Leaving him stretched out on the table, she let herself out of the room, closed the door as quietly as she could and went downstairs in search of Sandra.

Jessica found Sandra in the kitchen, her hands covered with a raw meat mixture and dozens of balls spread out on baking sheets across the granite-topped island in the center of the large kitchen. Cherry cabinets flanked stainless steel appliances and shiny copper pots hung from a rack above the island.

"Master said you would let me know what I needed to do on Friday."

Sandra rolled meat between her palms until it rounded into a ball. "You need to arrive by six. Make sure you wear stilettos, shiny ones." She tilted her head to one side. "That garter belt is fine, but your stockings should be black nylon or fishnet, preferably with a seam."

Jessica bit her lip and closed her eyes. They expected her to parade naked in front of other faculty. How many of her teachers would see her like this? A tear crept down her cheek. How could any of the faculty participate in such perversion?

"The first couple of hours you'll serve drinks as requested and pass trays of hors d'oeuvres. Later in the evening one of the professors probably will ask Master to take you into the dungeon. Master will let you know who has paid for your services."

Jessica tasted salt at the edge of her mouth. She swallowed hard and sniveled.

"It's not bad, really." Sandra's voice softened and Jessica wondered how long she had served the Professor. "At a party, most of them can't beat on you for more than a half hour before they wear out. When you get sent to their homes, they get to keep you all night. They're never allowed to have intercourse with you, they can only require that you service them orally."

Jessica put her head in her hands and sobbed. How much more could she endure? She should just give up on her education and go get a job behind the counter of a fast food chain or waiting tables at restaurant. No amount of money or prestige could be worth what she had suffered so far or what she faced at the end of the week.

She heard running water and looked up to see Sandra washing the meat off her hands. The woman dried them on a dish towel and then pulled Jessica into her arms. Her skin smelled of vanilla and her hair of apricots. Her small breasts pressed into Jessica's larger ones, making her long to caress them. Sandra ran her hands up and down Jessica's back, then tangled her fingers in her hair and kissed her. Both women's breathing got heavier.

Jessica pushed her groin against Sandra's and let her hand drift down the woman's back to her firm buttocks. She had wanted Sandra from the first time she had seen her kneeling at the Professor's feet. Her skin felt so delightful under Jessica's hand and her mouth tasted of peppermint and coffee.

Sandra thrust her tongue into Jessica's mouth and she sucked on it. Jessica whimpered when Sandra pulled her mouth away, but the woman traced the length of Jessica's neck with burning kisses. Jessica moaned and ground her pelvis into Sandra's. When Sandra licked Jessica's nipples, it almost made her come and she grabbed Sandra's rear with both hands as much to enjoy the feel of the flesh beneath her fingers as to keep her knees from buckling under her. She forgot about the party and any thoughts of abandoning the Professor.

Turning so Jessica backed up to the counter, Sandra put her hands on Jessica's waist and gave her a boost. Jessica released Sandra to put her hands on the edge and between the efforts of both of them, Jessica ended up sitting on the cold granite. Much to her delight, Sandra kissed her way down Jessica's chest and belly to the cleft between her legs. Jessica spread her thighs to allow Sandra unlimited access and gave herself up to the delights of the moment.

When Sandra thrust her tongue in between Jessica's nether lips and found her clit, Jessica convulsed in orgasm. She clapped one hand over her mouth to avoid screaming and kept her balance with the other. Sandra licked, sucked, and thrust her tongue deep into Jessica until she came again, her entire body shaking.

She heard heavy breathing from the kitchen entrance and smelled a hint of spice and leather, but Jessica no longer cared. For the first time since she had entered the Professor's house two weeks ago, Jessica felt sexy and desirable. Her body reverberated with the spasms and her only thoughts of the moment were how much she would enjoy switching places with Sandra. Pushing herself off the counter, Jessica stopped to kiss Sandra and tasted herself on the other woman's lips. She lowered her head to the lovely pert breasts and cupped one in her hand while she sucked on the nipple of the other, reveling in how wonderful they felt.

Although she had never made love to another woman before, Jessica had often fantasized about what it might be like. She masturbated to thoughts of another woman's caress more often than to memories of a man's touch. Now, rolling her tongue around Sandra's lovely nipple she found herself more turned on than she had ever been in her life.

She slipped to her knees and Sandra kicked one leg up on the counter exposing her labia to Jessica. For a moment, Jessica could only admire the lovely, moist pink folds and the delicious nub of a clitoris peeking out from its hood. The musky aroma drew Jessica's face toward Sandra and her tongue flicked out for her first taste of another woman. Jessica moaned, the sweet, pungent flavor was just so delicious. Sandra pulled Jessica's face against her and Jessica obligingly licked the length of the woman's slit. Then she settled down to concentrate on her clit, teasing it with her tongue, sucking on it with her lips, and nibbling on it with her teeth.

Sandra trembled and cried out and more of her sweet juices gushed all over Jessica's face. Attempting to lick them all up, Jessica managed to make Sandra come again. She wanted to try for a third when a male voice jerked her back into the reality of her location.

"Nice. Sandra." The Professor snapped his fingers. Sandra lowered her leg and stumbled over to him. She sank to her knees and took his limp cock in her mouth.

Torn between gratitude that Sandra had taken on the distasteful task of servicing the Professor and regret at the interruption of the wonderful experience the other woman had offered her, Jessica hung her head. Not knowing what else to do, Jessica opened her knees, put her hands on her thighs, and stayed in that position until she heard the Professor moan.

Chapter Nine

The first guest arrived at seven-thirty. By then, Jessica and three other coeds had baked five dozen meatballs, stuffed three dozen mushrooms, arranged crackers around wheels of brie and Camembert, wrapped globs of chicken ground with spices in squares of phyllo dough, and filled baked puff pastry shells with chocolate-flavored whipped cream. The smells of garlic, ginger, and butter permeated the kitchen.

Two other women had spent an hour and a half dusting and vacuuming the living and dining rooms. Jessica heard another vacuum running in the dungeon. Taking the coat of the first professor to arrive, Jessica was so grateful that she hadn't taken a class from him she ignored his hand caressing her backside. Throughout the first part of the evening, as she strutted between the kitchen and the front of the house with trays of treats and glasses, faculty pinched, slapped, and squeezed her rear and breasts. One man even bent over and bit her nipple, eliciting a gasp.

She took some comfort in the fact that none of her graduate instructors attended the party. She had taken undergraduate lectures from three of the professors, but given that those classes had more than two hundred students each, Jessica didn't worry that those men would recognize her. Fortunately, most of the faculty attending taught in other departments at the University. She sighed with relief every time another professor she didn't recognize arrived at the party.

Her feet ached from parading around in six-inch heels and Jessica longed to take off her shoes. Whenever she had the opportunity, she rubbed her arms, weary from carrying heavy trays around the room. Around ten o'clock, the Professor caught her eye and crooked his finger at her. She set her tray of canapes down on the glass dining room table, grateful to get rid of the weight. But walking over to where he stood with another instructor near the foyer filled her with dread. The Professor had a black leather leash in his hands and as soon as Jessica stood close enough, he clipped it to her dog collar and handed it to the man standing next to him. Jessica didn't recognize him from school, but she thought she remembered someone saying he taught chemistry.

The man turned and headed for the dungeon stairs, tugging on Jessica's leash until she followed him, too weary to resist, too numb to even cry. At the entrance to the dungeon, the man stopped in front of a dozen wooden lockers to one side of the door and opened one. He removed his jacket, tie, and shirt, revealing a muscular chest and arms. Folding his clothing, he set it on the shelf inside. He emptied his trouser pockets of cell phone, wallet, and keys, and placed those on top of his jacket. After closing the door, he removed the key and slipped that into his pants pocket. He picked up Jessica's leash and continued into the dungeon.

Several students had proceeded them. Two, tied to crosses, already had visible welts across their backs. Another, bound in rope, hung from the ceiling while a man swatted her with a cane every time she swung in front of him. Despite the warnings Jessica had received, she still found it difficult to absorb the reality of the scene in front of her.

The chemistry professor led Jessica over to an odd-shaped bench. He made her kneel on the two smaller padded arms and pushed at her until she leaned her stomach onto the larger, raised leather platform which was parallel to the floor. He fastened leather cuffs around her wrists and ankles and clipped those to eye bolts. Her rear stuck up in the air and her breasts and head hung down, her hair hiding her face. The helplessness and humiliation of her position swept over her, but she swallowed her tears.

The first blow made Jessica jump. She could feel a fresh welt rising across her buttocks. The man repeated the strike several times with a riding crop then switched to a polished wooden paddle. He made her count and thank him for every blow.

"That's fifty, Sir. Thank you, Sir." Jessica felt bruised and battered, the pain in her feet forgotten with the onslaught on her rear.

The man stepped around in front of her and lowered the zipper on his pants. He pulled out an erect penis and pushed it toward her lips. Jessica obediently opened just wide enough for him to slide inside and let her tongue stroke the underside. He reached down and grabbed her nipples between his thumbs and forefingers and pinched until Jessica released a muffled scream.

Moaning with pleasure, he thrust in and out of her mouth pulling on her nipples. He pushed so deeply down her throat she had difficulty not gagging. She concentrated on breathing through her nostrils and keeping her lips wrapped around him, hoping he wouldn't last long. He picked up the pace, thrusting his hips harder into her face. Jessica gurgled. When he finally exploded in her mouth, she swallowed, grateful that it meant the end of the aching in her jaw and the agony in her nipples. His semen didn't taste nearly as bad as the Professor's.

The man unclipped Jessica's wrists and ankles and helped her regain her feet. Then he sat down on the floor next to the bench and pulled her into his arms. He sat with her in his lap, his arms wrapped around her and her head nestled against his shoulder. Although she didn't understand why the man held her, Jessica found comfort in his embrace. One hand slid slowly up and down her back and she wriggled closer against his chest, grateful for a touch that didn't hurt.

He stroked her cheek with his other hand and it strayed down her neck to her breast. She flinched, but this time he caressed her gently and then leaned over and sucked on her sore nipple. Jessica was surprised to find his touch arousing. The man had soft brown hair, cut just above his ears, and a goatee sprinkled with grey. He lifted his mouth from her breast and looked at her with kindness in his dark eyes. She raised her chin and his lips locked on hers, his tongue finding its way deep into her mouth.

His hand moved from her breast down to her legs. Jessica clamped her knees together, but he wormed his fingers between her thighs. When he stroked her between her labia, she sighed and opened her legs to him. If it pleased him to get her off, she shouldn't object. Letting him play with her was much preferable than getting beaten by him. She sucked on his tongue while he thrust two fingers inside her, massaging her clit with his thumb. He kept at it until Jessica slid her hands around his neck and clung to him while her body convulsed, her cry filling his mouth.

He released her lips and removed his hand from between her legs, bringing his fingers to her mouth. She sucked her own juices off his fingers. Then he kissed her lightly on the forehead and nudged her off his lap. He unfastened her leash from her collar, handed it to her, and walked away. Jessica watched him disappear through the door in a daze, any illusions that their encounter held any meaning for him dashed.

Not knowing what else to do, she used the bathroom and then returned upstairs to the Professor. He took the leash from her, clipped it back to her collar, and handed it to a man with a long, hooked nose. She wanted to fall to her knees and beg the Professor to allow her to go home, but she knew instinctively that would only anger him. So she followed this man back to the dungeon.

He led her to a dental chair in the far corner of the dungeon and pushed her to sit down. She grimaced when her sore flesh touched the leather seat. He clamped restraints on the arms and legs of the chair around her wrists and ankles forcing her backside tightly into place which made her whimper. The man ignored her cry, slipped his arms into a lab coat, and opened the doors of a white metal cabinet next to the chair. Jessica trembled. She had never seen the contents of this particular piece of furniture and she feared what new torments it would enable.

The man pulled exam gloves over large hands then rubbed something cold over her breasts and chest with a gauze pad. The smell of disinfectant assaulted her nostrils. His almost white hair barely covered the top of his head and formed a short fringe around his scalp. When he looked up at her, she saw a wicked glint in his pale blue eyes.

The man wiped off whatever he had rubbed on her breasts and then swabbed them again with pads that smelled of iodine and left brown stains on her skin. He pulled another pair of exam gloves on over the first and turned away for a moment. When he faced her again, he held an inch and a half long needle with a plastic hub. He pulled off the protective tip, pressed that against one side of her nipple, and pushed the slender metal needle through her flesh. Jessica screamed. The man chucked and grabbed another needle. He put this one through her other nipple. Jessica panted in little gasps trying to pull air into her lungs.

The man leaned over and whispered in her ear. "Take long, deep breaths. It's easier to process the pain that way." He reached for another needle. This one he inserted above her areola piercing her skin in two places so about half the needle stuck out after going under her skin. One by one, he placed needles in her breasts until she had a column of needles rising up her chest. Jessica's breasts felt like they were on fire. The pain of each needle drove away the agony of the one that had gone in before, although the heat didn't dissipate.

He continued to stick needles into her, connecting the two columns on her breasts with a row of needles across her chest. Then he put a column between them. Jessica could no longer focus her eyes, the room and the man's face swimming in front of her. With her eyes half closed, her head dropped to her shoulder and her hair draped over her pierced flesh.

"Oh, no." The man put a gloved hand on either side of her head and lifted it upright. "Mustn't contaminate the field." He brought a metal band across Jessica's forehead and fastened it in place. The cold against her skin helped her regain her equilibrium, a little. But now she couldn't even move her head.

The man removed the gloves and dropped them into a wastebasket lined with a plastic bag. He pulled on another pair. Her head immobilized, Jessica could no longer see the pattern of needles across her chest and breasts. But she felt the heat where each piece of metal pierced her skin. The man flicked one needle, then another. Jessica cried out. He moved across the needles, jerking, jiggling, and jostling them until she screamed again. Once more she couldn't catch her breath. Just when she thought she had endured every torture known to man, she discovered the Professor's dungeon held even more ways to torment her.

Jessica heard a whir of machinery and the back of the chair lowered toward the floor. When it stopped, the man presented her with an erect penis protruding from the zipper in his slacks. She whimpered, but she turned her face toward him and opened her mouth enough so he could slide it in. He pushed into her face until her jaw ached and tears spilled from her eyes. Instead of coming in her mouth, he stepped back and spewed all over her face. She coughed, got some in her nose, and choked. She had never realized just how many ways men could humiliate women.

The man wiped her face clean with a paper towel and held a bottle of water to her lips. Jessica sipped at it, grateful for the relief from the heat that still tormented her breasts and chest. He kissed her on the forehead. Machinery whirred and the chair brought Jessica back to a sitting position. The blood draining from her head made her feel even weaker and only the metal across her forehead kept her chin off her chest.

She heard the snap of exam gloves as the man replaced the ones he wore yet again. When he removed the first needle, she cried out. The next few elicited sobs. Needle after needle pulled from her skin, brought back the pain to that spot and made her skin even hotter. After he had pulled all the needles out except the last two, he grabbed the tips of those and lifted her breasts by the needles in her nipples. Jessica screamed. He pulled away the plastic wrapping from a foot-long thin metal rod and used it to strike her impaled nipples over and over again until she lost consciousness.

Chapter Ten

Jessica woke in a dark room lying on a mattress covered with a smooth linen sheet. A quilt lay across her and she felt a warm body on either side. She drifted back to sleep and woke again when light penetrated around the edges of the curtains on the windows. Someone had an arm draped across Jessica's waist and she felt round, firm breasts pressed against her back. Long blond hair and the lovely curve of hips in front of her made her want to reach out and caress Felicia. Two other women lay on their sides in front of Felicia and Jessica looked over her shoulders and saw Sandra sleeping behind her on the king-sized bed.

Her rear still ached, but the pain and heat in her breasts and chest had subsided. Slowly, careful not to wake the others, she ran her fingers over the soft skin amazed that she could feel nothing where the needles had pierced it. Her stomach rumbled and she wondered how long she had slept. What time had the party ended? She remembered eating a couple of meatballs before the first guest arrived, but she hadn't had a meal since lunch the day before. Daylight outside in November meant it was at least seven o'clock. But, Jessica couldn't think of a way to extricate herself from the bed without waking the others.

She must have fallen asleep again, because the door to the room slammed open, jerking Jessica awake, and someone yanked the quilt off the bed. "Enough lollygagging." The

Professor's voice penetrated her sleep haze. "I want my breakfast and the rest of you have research to do."

One by one the women rolled off the bed. Jessica followed Sandra to a bathroom and waited for the opportunity to use the toilet. Then she stumbled into the kitchen, grateful to smell fresh-brewed coffee. Felicia disappeared with a tray and the rest of the students gathered around the counter to drink coffee, munch on leftovers from the party, and gossip about the men who had abused them. Jessica looked at the giggling women with whom she shared her morning brew. One brunette had bruises across her chest. Several had rope marks on their wrists and arms. Any time one of them turned her back, Jessica saw welts and stripes. She couldn't understand why they all seemed so cheerful, given what they had endured.

Felicia returned with an empty tray and a pile of twenties. She handed three to each of the women standing around the counter. Jessica stared at the money in her hand torn between thinking about what it could buy and the disgust for what it had cost her. Apparently the payment served as some sort of dismissal, because all the women except Felicia left the kitchen. She gathered up the cups, sealed up the rest of the leftovers, and returned them to the refrigerator. Jessica followed the other women to the foyer, where she found them putting on their clothing. She stuffed the bills in her jacket pocket and pulled on her bra, slip, skirt, and blouse.

Sticking her arms in the sleeves of her jacket and settling it on her shoulders, Jessica walked over to where Sandra stood with her hand on the front door knob. "What's with the money?"

"He always gives us a small cut of what the faculty pay to play with us." Sandra, smiled and opened the door. "Gotta get home and feed the cat." She planted a kiss on Jessica's cheek and left.

Jessica went back to the closet for her coat and then

followed the other women out of the house. She wobbled down the stairs on her stilettos and noticed that several of the other women carried theirs and wore more comfortable three-inch heels. Cursing under her breath for not having the foresight to do the same, Jessica limped to the bus stop, her feet aching with every step. Rush hour passengers crowded the bus and Jessica couldn't find a seat. She hung onto the overhead strap trying to take some of her weight on her arms.

"Miss, are you okay?" She looked down to see a young boy, no more than fifteen years old, sitting on one of the bench seats parallel to the sides of the bus.

"Just tired."

"Would you like my seat?" The boy rose.

Jessica dropped into it, managing not to cringe when the hard plastic came up against her tender rear, and rewarded the boy with her biggest smile. "Thanks a lot. My feet are killing me."

He looked down toward the floor. "If you don't mind my saying so, why do you wear those shoes?"

"My employer requires them and I forgot to bring a pair to change into." Jessica appreciated the boy's kindness, but she really didn't have the energy to engage in conversation, especially with a minor.

But he leaned down and whispered in her ear. "Are you a str... exotic dancer?"

She laughed and realized how bitter that sounded to her own ear. "No, I work for an eccentric professor." She hoped that would satisfy his curiosity and stop his questions.

He looked as if he wanted to ask more so she leaned her head back against the seat and closed her eyes. He got off a couple of stops later.

From her own bus stop, she hobbled toward her apartment, stopping at every bench, stoop, and anywhere else she could sit for a few moments to relieve the pain walking inflicted on her sore feet. The ten-minute walked dragged into twenty.

Each time she sat down, she sucked in her breath as her tender rear made contact with wood or cement.

Finally, she limped through the tiled lobby of her apartment and into the thankfully open elevator. While the car rose, she removed her shoes. Although walking in her stocking feet didn't hurt the balls and heels of her feet as much, it stretched out the tight muscles in her calf. She got off the elevator and leaned over to stretch out a little. Leaning one hand against the wall to steady herself, she carried her shoes in the other as she made her way to the refuge of her apartment. She closed the door behind her, stripped out of her clothing leaving a trail of discarded garments scattered throughout the apartment and headed for the bathroom.

She turned on the water taps, mostly hot with only a little cold to create the scalding temperature she normally enjoyed. Reaching for the lavender oil, Jessica saw the steam rising from the water that splashed out of the faucet. She didn't need to touch her ass to realize how the hot water would feel on her abused skin. She reached for the tap, turned off the hot water, and wait for the tub to finish filling with cold water.

Easing into the still warm water, she dropped her head beneath the surface for as long as she could hold her breath. She emerged, sat up, and wept until her shoulders shook and her breath came in loud, raspy gasps. She just had to think of some way to extricate herself from the mess she had gotten into.

The boy on the bus thought she stripped for a living. How much would that pay, she wondered? She wiped the back of her hands under her eyes. At least she wouldn't get beaten every couple of weeks and men would stick money in her g-string instead of needles in her breasts. "How bad could it be?" Her voice echoed in the tub enclosure. Jessica thought of the humiliation she would endure if someone from the University saw her on the stage.

At least those who attended the Professor's parties had as much reason as she to keep who and what they saw there confidential. Working as an exotic dancer might pay the bills, but it wouldn't exactly enhance her career options. In addition to starting over at some other university, she would give up the Professor's endorsement. After all she had suffered, that one promise prevented her from running away.

She dried her skin carefully with a soft towel, applied arnica to the bruises, and reached for a skirt but then withdrew her hand from the closet. Lifting her chin a little, she defiantly grabbed a pair jeans and a sweater before easing herself down into the chair in front of her desk. She found an e-mail from the Professor containing the documents with the faculty panel's approval of her proposal and the authorization to start her research. She just stared at the computer screen. Then she opened her browser to the newspaper's help wanted ads.

Jessica spent the next several days applying for employment online and in person. She found very few jobs listed and those required experience she didn't have. Even a position as a cashier in the supermarket asked for a resume in addition to requiring a filled-out application. She created several different versions of her resume, trying to write herself into something someone would hire. She even applied for a couple of credit cards, but got turned down. After a week, she gave up and put together a list of mental health clinics she could contact to get the data she needed for her research.

J

Most of Jessica's bruises had disappeared when she

received an e-mail instructing her to visit the Professor. After hanging her garments in his front closet, she found him in his office, fully clothed.

"Apparently Professor Branson enjoyed playing with you at the party. He's asked for you to visit him."

Jessica wondered whether that was the needles or the guy who made her come. Before she could think of an appropriate way to phrase the question, the Professor took several pieces of leather from his desk drawer and gestured for Jessica to join him on his side of the desk. He fitted a strap around her waist, the leather snug against her skin, and locked it in place with two small padlocks. He made her spread her legs and placed a second piece of leather between her legs. The hourglass shape covered both her openings.

Jessica didn't know whether to be grateful that the Professor wouldn't permit Branson to have sex with her or indignant at him taking possession of her genitals. While she fumed silently, the Professor attached straps from each end of the leather between her legs to the belt around her waist. He secured those with two additional padlocks and handed her a piece of paper with a North Shore address along with a computer-generated map and directions. "You can take the Miata. The keys are by the kitchen door. Return here when he releases you."

"Yes, Master. Thank you, Master."

"Oh, and don't bother getting dressed. Just put your coat on."

Jessica closed her eyes and swallowed. What if she got stopped by the police? "Yes, Master. Thank you, Master."

She drove from the Professor's house at five miles below the speed limit. At every stop sign she stayed for half a minute before pulling out, even if she saw no other traffic, and she braked for every yellow light. When she pulled into the driveway of Professor Branson's two-story brick house, her hands were shaking. She still didn't know if he was the needles or the riding crop. She sighed with relief when the tall, brown-haired man who had paddled her bottom, and not the one who stuck needles in her breasts, opened the door.

He took her coat off as soon as the door closed behind her and Jessica dropped to her knees. Pulling her hair back so her face tilted up toward him, he kissed her long and hard. Jessica found herself breathing heavily, despite the anticipation of the pain he would inflict on her. After a few minutes, he took her hand and led her up the stairs into a bedroom. A four-poster king-size bed with a black and grey comforter that matched the curtains, a leather wing-back chair, and a walnut chest of drawers were the only furniture in the room.

"Undress me."

"Yes, Sir. Thank you, Sir."

Jessica unbuttoned his blue, cambric shirt, and pushed it off his shoulders. She stepped behind him to remove it, folded it, and set it on the chair. She unbuckled his belt and unfastened his tweed slacks. She pulled them down to his ankles and waited while he stepped out of them. Folding them required a little more care so his wallet and cell phone wouldn't fall out. Lastly, she slipped his silk boxers over his hips and down his legs. His erection almost hit her in the eye.

After she added those to the top of his clothing, Jessica knelt in front of the professor. He stroked her hair, then pulled it back and kissed her again. His hand firmly entangled in her locks, he pulled her to her feet. When he released her, he took a coil of rope from the bed and ran the length of it through his hands. Turning her around to face away from him, he bound her hands behind her back. Then he laced the rope around her breasts, binding them tightly, and looped the rest of the rope between her legs, around her arms, and waist. Jessica felt like a macrame sculpture.

He stepped back and surveyed his handiwork, a smile playing across his lips. After kissing her again, he bent Jessica over the bed, her stomach across the comforter, her rear in the air. The riding crop stung. "That's one, Sir. Thank you, Sir."

After raising welts with the riding crop, he smacked them with a wooden paddle and then laid into her with his belt. Jessica found she could set aside the pain, especially knowing that no one else could abuse her when he finished. This time she counted to seventy-five before he jerked her up by her hair and thrust himself into her mouth. His fingers stayed tangled in her hair, pushing her face hard into his crotch, until he came in her mouth. Even that seemed routine and she no longer had to hide her reaction since she didn't really have one.

Removing the rope took almost as long as tying her up and he made Jessica coil it before he pulled her into his arms. He lay down with her on the bed and put her hand on his not-quite-flaccid penis. While she stroked him to erection, he squeezed one finger in between the leather panel covering her crotch and found her clit. He made her come three times. Although her body reacted to his caresses, her mind drifted off to think of other things: her research, Alyssa's husband, calling Louis to see if the house had sold and finding out if she had incurred additional debt as a result.

Professor Branson pulled her face back down to suck on him. This time, though, he let her move her mouth up and down at her own pace. Although it took him longer to get off, Jessica found it much less painful and easier to keep her mind occupied on anything but her current predicament. He held her in his arms on the bed for half an hour before he sent her back to the Professor.

Chapter Eleven

All Jessica could think of on the drive back to Professor Lawrence's house was her need to pee. Although she stopped carefully at the stop signs and stayed just below the speed limit, she accelerated rather than braked for yellow lights. Slamming the car door shut she minced her way up the walk and into the kitchen through the back door. Felicia stood over the sink, her hands immersed in soapy water.

"Where is Master?" Jessica pushed her thighs together, pressing the leather strap between her legs tight against her crotch.

"Not here." Felicia moved the pan she had scrubbed into the other side of the sink.

Jessica pressed her lips together for a moment. "I really need to pee."

Felicia rinsed the pan under the tap. "Key's right there." She jutted her chin toward the brass key rack nailed to the wall next to the door jamb. "Put the belt in Master's office. There's an envelope for you on his desk."

Jessica grabbed the small key from the rack and fumbled with the lock attaching the belt between her legs to the one around her waist as she stumbled toward the powder room off the kitchen. She lifted the belt out of the way to sit down, deciding she could wait to remove the rest. For a minute, her body betrayed her and she couldn't get anything out.

When she finally did start, everything poured out of her and her relief felt almost orgasmic. She sat for a few minutes recovering before flushing the toilet and washing her hands.

After removing the rest of the locks and laying the belt across his chair, Jessica spotted a cream-colored linen envelope on the Professor's desk with her first name on it written in all small letters. Inside she found three twenty-dollar bills and a sticky note. "I expect a detailed research plan by end of next week," it said in the Professor's precise handwriting. Jessica took a deep breath. That would require forty or fifty hours of work. Hopefully, if he expected that, he would not require any other services of her until she completed his assignment. At any rate, if he allowed her time to heal between visits to other faculty, he couldn't send her to anyone else for at least a week.

Still that wouldn't prevent her from meeting his needs should he require that of her. Bile rose in her throat, Jessica put a hand over her mouth, and rushed to the bathroom off the front hallway. But when she leaned over the porcelain bowel, her stomach heaved and nothing came out. Of course she hadn't eaten since lunch and, she looked at her watch, it was now past midnight. She went to the sink and splashed cold water on her face. Looking in the mirror, she stared at the chain links encircling her neck. She found it interesting that she could disassociate herself from everything that happened at Professor Branson's house, but the mere thought of servicing Professor Lawrence made her ill.

Her stomach rumbled and Jessica wandered back into the kitchen. "Are there any leftovers available, please, Felicia?"

The blonde rinsed her hands under the tap and dried them on a dishtowel. She opened the refrigerator, pulled out a small glass dish covered in plastic wrap, set it on the counter, gave Jessica a smile, and returned to the sink. Jessica pulled back the moisture covered wrap to find rigatoni in meat sauce. The lightness in her head won out over the queasiness in her stomach and she pulled a clean fork from the dish rack. She thought about warming the food in the microwave, but decided the cold pasta would probably go down easier.

"Do you want me to wash this," she asked after she had emptied the bowl.

"Just leave it, I'll take care of it later. Go ahead and get dressed and I'll drive you home. Did you leave the key with the chastity belt?" Felicia rinsed out the sink with the spray nozzle and dried her hands again.

"Yes, Ma'am."

"We're not allowed to address each other that way. Only female dominants and faculty get called Ma'am." Felicia headed out to the foyer and Jessica followed.

While Jessica put on her clothing, Felicia slipped into her trench coat, buttoned it and cinched the belt around her narrow waist.

"Do you live here, then?" Jessica stuck the envelope in her pocket and buttoned her coat.

"More or less." Felicia smiled, opened the front door and locked it behind them. "I have an official address elsewhere, but I only stop in there once or twice a month to check on things."

Felicia's light tone took Jessica aback. "You like it?"

Felicia climbed into the Miata, reached over and unlocked the passenger door. "What's not to like?" she asked when Jessica climbed in. "I have a lovely place to live, a fun car to drive, and I can take any classes I want." She started the car, put it in gear, and backed out of the driveway. "I can go to school forever if I choose, I'll never have to work as long as I please Master and take care of his house."

Jessica fingered the envelope in her pocket. "But, he's so cruel."

"Oh, he's really a sweet old guy at heart. Yes, he's a a sadist, but since I'm a masochist that works out rather well."

"And taking abuse from other faculty?"

Felicia shrugged her shoulders and smiled. "I'm a slut. I love the attention. So do most of the other girls. You're one of three that he's taken in since I've known him who didn't beg for the opportunity to serve. Not sure why he bothers, really. He turns students down every term."

The concept that someone could actually enjoy serving the Professor and would beg for the opportunity left Jessica at a loss. She gave up trying to make conversation during the rest of the drive.

J

Jessica lay on her stomach, letting the air in Professor Branson's bedroom cool the heat on her sore behind. He waited exactly ten days, Professor Lawrence's minimum, between requests for her. With liberal applications of arnica, her backside usually felt normal for two or three days before she had to present it to him for abuse again.

"You know, if you came over here on your own, I could see you more often." He lay on his side next to her, alternately stroking her back and playing with her hair. "You wouldn't have to wear this." He tugged at the belt around her waist. "And we could have real sex."

Jessica kept her face in the crook of her arm to avoid voicing her thought: What makes you think I want to have real sex with you? Although she found Bryce Branson attractive, she had no interest in having a relationship with a man who got sexually turned on by bruising her bottom.

"If you're not interested in having an affair with me..." he brought his mouth to her ear and his hot breath made her shiver, "there's always money. How much of the three hundred dollars I pay for your visits does Lawrence give you anyway?"

Every muscle in Jessica's body clenched and her eyes widened at the outrageous percentage. She rolled onto her side so she faced Bryce. "You pay three hundred dollars for me to come over here for four hours?"

He stared into her eyes and teased her nipples with his thumb. She interpreted that as a positive response.

"My ass can't take your abuse any more often. What would you want if I came over in between?"

Bryce leaned over and sucked one nipple into his mouth, chewing on it until she gasped, then lifted his head. "I want to fuck you long and hard. If you can take it rough, I don't have to blister your butt."

"And you'd pay me three hundred dollars?" She reached for him, stroking his sticky length until it jumped into her hand.

"If you'd spend the night, I'd pay you five hundred."

Jessica closed her eyes. Almost one month's rent. She touched the links of the chain around her neck. The Professor had already turned her into a prostitute. Bryce just offered her the opportunity to eliminate the pimp and collect all the money for herself.

"He doesn't have to know." Bryce misinterpreting her fiddling with her collar, pulled her against his chest and wrapped his arms around her. "I would still ask for you every ten days and I would still blister your butt during those sessions. But if you'll come in between, I would settle for rough sex. Especially if you'll role play." He yanked her hair back and kissed her hard, thrusting his tongue in her mouth.

"Role play?" she asked when he released her.

"I like play-rape, especially if you can pretend you're someone else like the little girl to my daddy, the prisoner to my cop, the student to my teacher." He nibbled on her ear.

"I think I've got that last one down pretty well." She let one hand slide down his side to his hip and brought it around to tease him with her fingers. If the man was willing to pay five hundred dollars to spend the night with her, she could at least let him think she found the idea appealing.

"No, I was thinking more of plaid skirt, bobby socks, and pigtails." His breathing got heavier.

"You supply the wardrobe and I can be anyone you want." She gripped him in her hand, squeezing just until he moaned with pleasure. Those acting classes she had taken as an undergrad just might come in handy.

J

On her way home from Professor Lawrence's house, Jessica's wondered how Professor Branson could afford a thousand dollars a week for her company. The revelation that the department chair supported his lavish lifestyle by pimping out his research assistants, made her suspicions. When she arrived at her apartment, she went online to purchase another background check. This time the cost didn't hurt as much. Even at only sixty dollars every ten days, Bryce's interest in her had already eased her financial straits somewhat.

She found this background check more useful as well. Apparently, before taking a position at the University, Professor Branson had worked at a pharmaceutical firm. He had several lucrative patents in his name and they probably still brought him a significant income. Jessica couldn't fathom why someone like that would accept a low-paying position as a college professor. She shrugged. Drug money paid her bills just as well as money from any other source.

Three days later, Bryce sent her an e-mail with a description of the role he expected her to play and the scenario he envisioned. When she arrived at his house, Jessica found the door unlocked and a maid's uniform waiting for her in the front closet. The short black skirt revealed the garters holding up her stockings and the plunging neckline almost exposed her areola. She tied the tiny white apron around her waist and pinned the starched cap in her hair with the bobby pins attached to it.

With a feather duster in one hand and a broom in the other, she minced up the stairs and down the hall. When she passed Bryce's bedroom, he flung the door open, grabbed her by the hair and dragged her inside. Even though she had expected his assault, it still took her by surprise and she reacted instinctively. Dropping broom and duster, she used both hands to try and push him away. He tossed her on the bed, so she rolled away before he could jump on top of her. She almost made it out of the room when he grabbed her hair again, forcing her to stop. This time he pushed her on the bed and landed on top of her. While she tried to push him off, he buckled restraints he had attached to the bedposts around her wrists. He clamped his mouth over hers and thrust his tongue deep into her mouth, despite her attempt to clench her teeth against his assault.

Even knowing she would get paid well for the scene, a part of Jessica panicked. She struggled, but the weight of his body, combined with the cuffs around her wrists and ankles, kept her helpless. Releasing her mouth, Bryce sat up and pulled off his t-shirt and boxers. He put one large hand on the fabric covering each of her breasts and ripped her dress away. Jessica shook her head and renewed her struggles, even though she knew they were in vain.

Bryce squeezed one nipple between his thumb and fore finger and bit down on the other while she wriggled beneath him. Although it hurt, the pain didn't compare to what she experienced when he beat her. She pushed the panic away and relaxed. Might as well enjoy this. Besides if she didn't, he would hurt her more than he did with his paddle. She let the thought of taking it between her legs instead of in her mouth arouse her enough to evoke moisture.

Still, when Bryce tried to get between her legs, Jessica clamped her knees together. After all, he paid good money for her to resist him. Bryce pried her thighs apart with one hand and jammed himself inside her, hard. He pounded into her, hammering her until she ached and he had a sheen of sweat across his forehead.

"Please, Monsieur, I'm begging you to stop." Jessica faked a French accent as best she could. She tried to pull away from the onslaught between her legs, but between her restrained wrists and his weight on her, she really couldn't move.

Still her attempts at struggling seemed to have the desired effect. His pace picked up and his face contorted. With a loud groan he jammed himself all the way up inside her and she could feel him spasming. When he finally pulled out of her and flopped over on his back, Jessica glanced at the clock on the wall across the room and realized he had kept at it for an hour. She decided she would rather have him paddling her backside than try to accept him in her mouth for that long.

They lay panting next to each other. His sweat evaporating off her body chilled Jessica and she shivered. Bryce unbuckled the restraints, pulled her into his arms and kissed her with a tenderness that surprised, her enough to kiss him back. He laced his fingers into her hair, but didn't tug on it. Instead, he stroked her back and kissed her neck. Under his unexpectedly gentle touch, Jessica's breathing grew heavier and she wrapped her arms around her neck. He brought his leg up between her knees and let her rub against him. She could feel him growing hard against her stomach.

Her desire ignited, she squeezed him until he was fully erect and raised up to take him inside her. He chuckled and let her ride him, massaging her breasts and flicking at her nipples with his thumbs. When building orgasm made it impossible for her to stay upright, Bryce grabbed her behind and thrust his hips upward until she exploded and collapsed on his chest. Then, he rolled her over on her back, moved so he lay perpendicular, and pumped into her for what seemed like forever until he filled her again with his semen.

Jessica looked at the time and pushed herself to the edge of the bed. Bryce grabbed her. "What's your hurry?"

"The last bus leaves in twenty minutes." She tried to pull his hands apart, but he had locked them together.

"I'll drive you home." He pulled her back onto the bed.

"I'd rather not..."

"I'll drop you off at the nearest bus stop. I don't need to know exactly where you live, but I don't want you traipsing around by yourself at this time of night."

Jessica stared at the man stretched out next to her. Although in some ways he abused her as much as Professor Lawrence, he also seemed to genuinely care about her well-being. He certainly showed her a great deal more affection than Professor Lawrence did and she wondered if this was how the Professor treated Felicia. She relaxed and let Bryce wrap his arms around her. The next thing she knew daylight flooded the room through the open windows and she could hear water running in the bathroom. Bryce had covered her with the quilt.

When she opened the bathroom door, steam rolled out to greet her and she could smell Old Spice shaving cream. Bryce turned off the water, stepped out of the shower, and wrapped a towel around his waist. "All yours, my dear." He bowed from the waist and swept a hand toward the shower. "When you get dressed, I'll take you out to breakfast."

Jessica stepped inside the shower and pulled the clear glass doors closed. "Probably not a good idea, what if someone sees us and lets Professor Lawrence know? Probably best if I just take the bus home."

"If you insist." He rubbed his hair with another towel.

He might offer a bit more gallantry than the Professor, Jessica thought, but she still only provided sexual entertainment and meant nothing more to him than that.

Chapter Twelve

At the beginning of fall term the following August, Professor Lawrence summoned Jessica to his house on a Saturday afternoon. Previously, she had never arrived at his home before six in the evening. When he wanted to see her in the daytime, he had her come to his office on campus.

Walking from the bus stop to the Professor's house, Jessica ran every possible reason he could want her to appear at this unusual time through her mind. He couldn't find fault with her appearance. She had shaved two days before, her black stockings had a seam along the back of her leg, she wore no panties under her linen skirt. If he had planned a party, Felicia would have given her the date a week ago. She chewed the inside of her lip.

What if the Professor rejected her data as invalid? Jessica had completed her research. She hoped to finish her dissertation, and get free of him, in less than six months. If he made her collect additional data or worse, start over, she would have to endure even more months of hell as his slave.

Her eyes widened. What if he had found out about her unauthorized visits with Bryce? Two months after Bryce persuaded her to spend time with him that Professor Lawrence didn't know about, Jessica had purchased a used blue Mustang convertible. Although she drove everywhere else, grateful to minimize the time she spent on public transportation, Jessica still took the bus to Professor Lawrence's house so he wouldn't ask how she could afford a car. Bryce had given her a remote for his garage door so no one would see a car parked in his driveway when she visited him. They never went anywhere together and Bryce still asked the Professor to send her to visit every ten days.

In between, Bryce would e-mail Jessica every few days with a description of which role he wanted her to play. She would obediently drive to his house, arriving to find the appropriate outfit awaiting her. It amazed her that Bryce never seemed to run out of new scenarios. Of course, they always had one thing in common — him pretending to rape her while she tried unsuccessfully to fight him off.

Jessica had made sure her secret visits didn't interfere with her schoolwork. She couldn't imagine how the Professor could have learned of their trysts. By the time she climbed up the steps to the Professor's home, Jessica's stomach churned. Her shaking hands made it difficult to remove her clothing. In his office, instead of waiting for her to kneel on the floor, the Professor told her to sit down and pointed to a chair.

Warily, Jessica eased herself down onto the leather, cool against her naked skin. She gripped the arms.

"An unusual situation has developed." The Professor laced his hands together over his leather desk blotter. "One of the professors who joined the faculty this term has approached me about his interest in domination and submission."

Jessica tilted her head to one side, wondering what made that unusual. New faculty always seemed to learn quickly that Professor Lawrence could fill any kinky needs they had.

"This gentleman is a submissive and he would like me to find him a FemDom."

Jessica's eyes widened and she swallowed hard. For the first time since the Professor coerced her into giving herself to him, he mentioned something about domination and submission that appealed to her. She so longed to take control, to put others on their knees, to hurt someone.

"Unfortunately, he only wants to serve a brunette, the darker the better, which rules out Felicia and Sandra. I do believe you have the potential to learn what is needed to meet this man's needs."

Jessica gripped the arms of the chair. A picture of Professor Lawrence tied to a cross while she lashed his back with a flogger flashed through her mind and the thought made her tremble with delicious anticipation. She pressed her lips together to avoid smiling at the thought.

Professor Lawrence handed Jessica a slim, black paperback with stark white letters spelling out FemDom 101 by Lady da Sade. She stared at the book, the title offering a promise of freedom and control. "You can start with this. Read in the living room. Take notes." He pushed a yellow legal pad and a ballpoint pen across the desk. "When you're done, I'll answer any questions you have and take you down to the dungeon for your first training session."

"Yes, Master. Thank you, Master." For the only time since she had first forced those words out of her mouth, they actually meant something to her beyond the required platitudes.

J

Jessica loved everything about dominating that she hated about submitting. The Professor used Felicia and Sandra to train her in flogging, rope bondage, candle wax, needle play, and use of a single tail. She took great pleasure in inflicting pain on two of those who had tormented her so much those first few days. Unfortunately, they both seemed to enjoy everything she did to them. She could only long for an opportunity to hurt the Professor.

He brought in one of his male students to teach her cock and ball torture, which he referred to as CBT. On the one hand, she regretted not getting to hurt the Professor. On the other, she really didn't want to touch his genitals for any reason, even to torture them, if she didn't have to.

The Professor's boy had silky blond hair that grazed his shoulders and blue eyes that looked at Jessica with adoration. He had shaved his muscular chest and arms and removed all the hair from his groin and buttocks. Sandra showed Jessica how to attach clothespins to the boy's scrotum without damaging his testicles. Jessica experimented with a variety of sensations on the boy — the Wartenberg wheel, ice, candle wax, ball crushers, miniature floggers. To her surprise, he stayed hard as a rock no matter how much she hurt his genitals. Despite the pain she inflicted, he just stared at her with a reverent look in his eyes that made Jessica melt.

She knew better than to ask the Professor for permission to have the boy lick her. But her arousal made her realize that, just like Bryce and the Professor's other faculty friends, she got turned on by physically hurting someone. That thought sobered her at first. Then she worried about how frustrated she might get if she had to torture a man without any hope of relief because of the chastity belt. And how would a submissive react if he found the woman he paid to dominate him wearing such a device?

After the boy left, she approached the Professor in his office. "I cannot go to a submissive locked in chastity."

He raised one eyebrow. "You can't have sex with him."

"Of course not, but I will require him to worship me orally." She jabbed one finger at the cover of the book that still sat on the Professor's desk. "And what if he wishes to participate in water sports?" The irony of discussing how she would Domme another professor while on her knees before the man who forced her to wear his collar did not escape Jessica.

Professor Lawrence leaned his head back and laughed. "I see I chose wisely in selecting you to dominate Professor Ross."

"Yes. But I will not agree to do so for such a small percentage of what you're paid. Also, I will expect you to absorb the costs of the wardrobe I will need." Jessica stiffened, awaiting retribution for her insolence.

The Professor let out a long sigh. "I will pay for suitable clothing for you to wear to your encounters with Thomas Ross. However, the percentage will remain the same. Fortunately for you, I can get more for you as a FemDom than I can as a submissive. You'll get a hundred-twenty for each encounter."

Jessica looked up to see that although the Professor did not smile at her, neither did she see the scowl that usually accompanied poor scholastic performance or disobedience. She grabbed at the opportunity these new circumstances offered. "How often will Professor Ross wish to see me?"

"Depends on how well you perform." He emphasized the last word.

"If he wishes to see me regularly you will have to tell Professor Branson I'm no longer available." Which would mean an extra four hundred dollars every other week, assuming he wanted sex with her bad enough to forgo beating her. "I can't exactly show up as a Domme with bruises all over my backside."

The Professor's nostrils flared. "Then I guess you'll provide excellent domination for Professor Ross, won't you?"

She lowered her eyes. "Yes, Master. Thank you, Master." Although she maintained the required subservient demeanor, she wanted to shout with glee. The unwitting Professor Ross offered a way out of the humiliation and torment she had suffered for the past ten months. She would make sure he was a very satisfied little boy.

J

Jessica arrived at Professor Ross's house wearing a tight, short, leather skirt, a leather bustier, suspender hose, a lace thong, knee-high boots with four-inch heels, and elbow-length leather gloves under her new leather trench coat. She had purchased a brass key to hang from her collar to make it look more like a necklace and she carried a leather duffle filled with things from the Professor's dungeon that she could use to hurt someone.

When she rang the bell, the door opened and she stepped inside. The man who closed the door behind her stood six inches taller than Jessica's five-foot, nine. Built like a football player, he had short grey hair receding from a widow's peak and a rugged face Jessica thought probably had once been quite handsome. He wore only a leather thong and dropped to his knees on the slate floor as soon as he had locked the front door.

She slapped his face. "Who told you you could wear a thong, you little worm."

"Yes, Mistress. I'm sorry, Mistress. May I take it off?"

Jessica sucked in her breath. She couldn't believe how much those few words turned her on. She placed her boot heel in the middle of the man's chest and pushed until he fell over on his side. "Do so immediately."

Tom pushed the thong down his hips without changing his position. He got it down to his ankles then reached behind to pull it off.

Good, still limber enough to hog tie. When the Professor had told her Tom's age, Jessica had wondered what kind of physical limitations he might have, even though Professor Lawrence said Tom had no medical issues she needed to worry about. She dropped her bag on him and it rolled off onto the floor with a clunk. "What room have you prepared for me?"

The man raised himself up on his hands and knees and kissed first one then the other of Jessica's boots. "I have a spare room upstairs with a cage and a St. Andrew's cross, Mistress. Would you like me to hang up your coat?"

With deliberate slowness, Jessica untied her belt and undid the buttons. She slipped off the coat and dropped it over the man's face. Then she sashayed up the stairs. She turned back about halfway up and watched him hang her coat in the closet. He started up the stairs with her bag in his hand.

"Who said you could stand up, boy?" That Tom appreciated her humiliation became obvious. Despite his age, apparently he could still get an erection. And Jessica continued to marvel at how much she was enjoying their encounter.

Tom dropped to his knees and scooted toward the stairs still holding her bag.

"Get on all fours and carry my bag in your teeth like the dog you are." She continued to the top of the stairs and watched him try to lift the heavy bag from stair to stair with his mouth. Jessica grinned. After months of torment by the Professor and his colleagues, she so enjoyed holding this end of the leash.

When he finally made it to the top of the stairs, Jessica let Tom lead her to the room at the far end of the hall. It did indeed hold a five- by three-foot black metal cage, a six-foot tall X-shaped cross and nothing else.

"Do you expect me to stand on my feet all evening, worm?"

"No, Mistress. So sorry, Mistress. May I stand to carry a chair in here, Mistress?"

"Yes, and bring a table, too, so I have a place to set my tools."

Tom scurried out of the room and returned carrying a

cherrywood Queen Anne chair with a plush white seat. He hurried back out to bring in a carved oak end table which he placed next to the chair then set the leather duffle on top of it. Jessica unzipped the side pocket and extracted a metal studded leather dog collar with a leather leash hooked to the D ring in the front. She snapped her fingers and pointed to her feet. Tom dropped to his knees in front of her and Jessica fastened the collar around his neck.

"Thank you, Mistress."

She took the handle of the leash, led the boy over to the cross, and tugged until he stood upright. Returning to the duffle, she extracted four leather cuffs from the main compartment. Buckling those around Tom's wrists and ankles, she clipped him to the hooks at the top and bottom of the cross. She ran one gloved hand over his still fairly firm buttocks and noticed his erection had gotten bigger. Good, she thought. The more he enjoys this, the more likely he is to ask for repeat visits. Grabbing the flogger from her bag, she ran the tails through her hand. Then she stepped back and threw them at his rear, just hard enough to sting a little.

"That's one, Mistress. Thank you, Mistress."

His words made Jessica shiver with delight and she had to wait a moment to regain her poise before she could deliver the next blow.

"That's two, Mistress. Thank you, Mistress."

Gradually she increased the intensity until each strike left a dozen red welts across his skin. She marked his rear, his shoulders, his thighs. She let the flogger wrap around his hips and flail his penis which brought a scream of agony followed by:

"That's twenty-six, Mistress. Thank you, Mistress."

Her thong soaked, her legs shaking, Jessica wanted to hit him once for every time someone had struck her. But, she realized, his skin could not take any more. His words and actions indicated he had some experience, but apparently not enough abuse to toughen his skin. She could hope, if he enjoyed the evening as much as she did, she would have the opportunity to continue her revenge another day.

Although Jessica had endured every lash, every paddle stroke, every needle in agony, she knew most of the Professor's other slaves got high off the pain. Given that Tom's erection had never wavered, even when the flogger's tails hit his penis, she could assume he was a masochist.

Draping the flogger over her bag, Jessica stepped up close behind Tom and ran her gloved hands over his striped back. "Had enough, boy?"

"I think my back has, Mistress. Thank you, Mistress."

"Well your backside is the only thing that's going to get my attention today." Jessica squeezed his cheeks and was rewarded with a pained groan. Leave him wanting more. She unclipped his wrist and ankle cuffs, led him over to the cage, and made him lay with his chest across it. After clipping his wrists and ankles to the bars of the cage, Jessica retrieved a leather blindfold and secured it over his eyes.

She hiked up her skirt so she could step into the strap-on harness and attached a large purple dildo. She removed one leather glove, replaced it with an exam glove, and covered two fingers with lube, the cold penetrating the rubber. Spreading his cheeks with her left hand, she eased her slick fingers inside and massaged his prostate. He groaned again and twitched.

Jessica withdrew and smeared lube all over the dildo before guiding the silicone phallus into him with one hand, bracing herself against his hip with her other. His moan started when it first touched him and continued until she slid it all the way in. She pulled back slowly until all but the tip had emerged and then thrust her hips forward and pushed it in as far as it would go. She rode him until her legs started shaking with need.

Pulling the dildo out with a slurpy pop, she ripped off

her strap-on harness and thong, peeled off the exam glove, unclipped the boy's wrists and ankles, and dragged him by the leash over to the chair. She placed the heels of her boots on his back and yanked his face in between her legs. He needed no further prompting, but pushed forward until his tongue found her wet slit. He licked the length of her and settled on her clit, nuzzling it until she exploded in his mouth. Grabbing a hunk of his hair in each hand, she tugged his mouth tighter against her and held it there until he licked and sucked her to three more orgasms.

She had no idea which turned her on more: taking control of a professor, who being bigger and stronger could easily overpower her, or having the freedom to abuse someone with the instruments that had been used to torture her. Jessica decided it didn't really matter.

Sated, she moved her boots forward and pushed Tom's shoulders away with the pointed heels. She allowed him to lick her boots from the point of the toe to the tip of her heel. When every inch of the leather glistened with his saliva, she stood, and straightened her skirt. She removed his blindfold, cuffs, and collar and put them with the flogger and the strap-on harness into her duffle.

She pointed to the dildo. "Take that, wash it off, and bring it back so I can put it away."

"Yes, Mistress. Thank you, Mistress." Tom took the end that she had attached to the harness in his teeth and crawled out of the room. He returned shortly after and held up the dildo for her to remove it from his mouth. "Is Mistress pleased with my service?" Tom sat back on his knees, rear on his heels, hands on his thighs palms facing upward. "Perhaps pleased enough to offer a small reward?"

Jessica stepped forward, put one foot between his thighs and brought the toe of her boot down on his erection. He screamed, but didn't go flaccid or try to pull away. She wanted to crush the life out of his penis to avenge herself for every one she had been forced to suck. But she restrained herself and pressed him against the wooden floor until he came with a shout, spurting onto her heel. She picked up her foot and stuck it in his mouth to clean off. When he finished, she grabbed his hair and pushed his face forward into the puddle on the floor. "Clean up your mess, boy." While he lapped at the floorboards, she left the house floating in a euphoria unlike anything she had ever known before.

Chapter Thirteen

Alyssa watched Jessica strut jauntily through the restaurant toward her table and smiled. For the first time in months, her young friend appeared sure of herself. Jessica held her head high and shoulders back. Her lovely dark hair shone against her pale skin and she had applied her makeup with the care that Alyssa had noted when they first met but which had been missing since her father's funeral.

"Hello, dear, you're looking lovely." Alyssa stood and embraced Jessica. The young woman gave her an enthusiastic hug.

"Thanks." Jessica floated into the chair the maitre d' pulled out for her. "How are you doing?"

"I'm fine, of course. How's your dissertation coming?"

Jessica picked up the menu. "I've made a lot of progress. I've completed all my research, compiled most of my data, and as soon as I get my professor to sign off on the results, I can start writing."

"And what's this?" Alyssa reached over and touched a necklace of stainless steel links that encircled the younger woman's neck. Although it resembled a slave collar, many young people just liked how they looked. This one had a brass key dangling from a center link instead of a small lock.

For a moment, Jessica's eyes widened and she put her

hand to her throat where she had left the top two buttons of her blouse undone.

"Can I get you ladies something to drink?" A lovely blond boy, not more than twenty-five, stood at Alyssa's elbow, order pad in hand.

"I'll have a glass of the house Chardonnay."

Jessica glanced at the wine list. "A glass of the Pouilly Fuisse white burgundy."

The boy left to get their wine and Jessica studied the menu, the unanswered question hanging in the air. After he returned and took their lunch orders, Alyssa raised her glass. "Here's to your continued academic success."

Jessica took a sip and set her glass down. She touched the links around her neck and leaned forward. "My professor is also my Master. I've served him for a just about a year now. Recently he's trained me to Domme and I've had another professor serving me." She looked up and her eyes shone with a gleam Alyssa knew too well.

"That's lovely, dear. I take it from your expression you prefer the dominant role?" Because of Jessica's odd reaction to questions about William Lawrence, Alyssa had suspected that the girl had gotten involved in BDSM some time ago. She was glad Jessica finally felt comfortable enough to confide in her.

Jessica nodded.

"I think it's best to start as a bottom, myself. I served an old guard master for several years before I started my training as a Domme." Alyssa wondered if the fact that she served her professor had kept Jessica from sharing this part of herself before.

Jessica's shoulders relaxed and she fingered the links. "I wondered about the necklace I've seen your husband wear."

"He's not my husband, dear." Alyssa took a sip of wine, enjoying the smokey vanilla flavor. "He's my slave. I've owned him for eighteen years now." She had married Klark so his employer would pay for her health insurance and to make it easier for her to have control over all their finances. But, she never thought of him as her spouse.

The young woman's bright green eyes widened. "How long ..." She twirled her wine glass. "I mean, when did you..."

"I met Master Chris shortly after I dropped out of school the first time, when I was twenty. I served him for five years. During the last two he brought in additional slaves — one female and one male — and trained me as their Mistress. When he felt I had sufficient training, and after determining I really had no interest in either submitting or bottoming, he released me from his collar." Although she had great respect for Chris and had kept in touch with him over the years, Alyssa had rejoiced when he removed his collar from around her neck.

The waiter set a plate of romaine lettuce topped with cucumbers, Gorgonzola crumbles, avocado slices, walnuts and ripe olives in front of her. Alyssa trickled honey mustard dressing from a small stainless pitcher over her salad. He held a foot-long oak pepper grinder above the plate. Alyssa nodded, then raised her hand when a light dusting of black flakes decorated the yellow dressing. When the waiter left, she continued. "I tried working as a pro for a few years." Alyssa speared a cheese-covered cucumber slice and a few lettuce leaves with her fork. "But, I didn't have much control. Men gave me money in expectation that I would meet their needs. If they didn't like what I offered, they took their money elsewhere. When I met Klark, I discovered the true beauty and symbiosis of a D/s relationship. I quit working and moved in with him. A year later, I collared him and he's served me faithfully ever since." She put the fork full of salad into her mouth and enjoyed the contrast between the tang of the cheese and the sweetness of the dressing.

"Symbiosis?" Jessica looked up from her plate of shrimp scampi on angel hair pasta.

Alyssa pulled off the gold signet ring she wore on her left index finger, Klark's gift to her at his collaring ceremony. She smiled affectionately at the memory. "Have you ever seen this symbol?

Jessica shook her head.

"The BDSM emblem, worn on the right if you're a submissive on the left if you're Dominant." Alyssa traced the three tear shapes inside the metal circle, thinking about how they defined not only her relationship but her life. "These represent the BDSM threesomes: bondage and discipline, domination and submission, and sadism and masochism, but also safe, sane, consensual, and tops, bottoms, switches. The curved lines can symbolize a lash as it swings, or the hazy border between where one of those threesomes ends and the other begins. The black fields of each section denote our controlled dark side. The metallic outlines stand for the chains of servitude and the circle surrounds them to embody the overlying unity within the community."

She handed the ring to Jessica who examined it for a moment and asked, "Why the holes?"

Alyssa accepted the ring back and returned it to her finger. "The holes show how any individual is incomplete without partners within the BDSM context." After all these years, she couldn't even imagine a life without Klark. "That's what I meant by symbiosis. I am a Dominant, a Mistress. But without my slave I have no one to serve me, no one to make me complete. Klark is a slave, but without a Mistress to serve his life has no purpose, no meaning. We fill each other's needs in a relationship that others might view as parasitic."

Jessica stirred pasta with her fork sending the smell of garlic wafting across the table. "What needs are those?"

"The primary ones are his need to serve against my need to control him." Alyssa sipped her wine thinking about how that didn't begin to touch the complexity of their relationship. "But, it can be as mundane as his need to have someone else manage his finances and my need to not clean house or do laundry."

"Do you hurt him?" Jessica whispered, her eyes glued to her plate.

"Yes. I am a sadist. Fortunately, he's a masochist so hurting him is something I do for our mutual pleasure." Alyssa paused to enjoy a few bites of her salad. "But, S&M isn't the basis of our relationship. He has given himself to me with no reservations. He obeys me without question. He serves me by earning the money that pays my mortgage and buys my food. He cleans my house, does my laundry, cooks my meals. He worships me as his Goddess." Alyssa took a long sip of her wine and thought about how fortunate she felt to have found Klark. The Internet had perverted the lifestyle, permitting those with no experience to claim dominant status and men pretending to be submissives to fulfill their sexual fantasies without offering anything in return.

"In exchange, I make sure he's cared for. I choose what food he eats, what clothes he wears, whether or not he gets to wear boxers or ladies underpants under his trousers. My domination and his submission form the foundation of our relationship. The sadism and masochism are spice when we have time and I'm so inclined."

Jessica brought a shrimp to her mouth with her fork. She bit off the meat and delicately removed the tail with her bright red fingernails. "Do you have sex with him?"

Alyssa laughed, then lowered her voice. "You mean besides allowing him to worship me orally and taking him with a strap-on?" She didn't wait for a response from Jessica. She suspected her friend had already gotten a taste of those activities. "For many FemDoms that's the extent of the sexual interaction they allow their slaves. But, I enjoy intercourse too much to give it up."

Jessica turned her fork round and round in her pasta. She lifted the strands to her lips, but then returned the fork to her plate. "Why do you make him wear women's underwear?"

Alyssa shrugged. "I make him wear more than that. I often take him out as my girlfriend Klaryce.

Jessica gasped.

"Yes, dear, that was Klark at Ed Debevic's six weeks ago. He does pass nicely, doesn't he?" Alyssa smiled.

"She looked so lovely. Her hair, makeup, so perfect." Jessica filled her mouth with pasta stifling, Alyssa suspected, the comparison between Klaryce's femininity and her own.

"To answer your question, I use feminization both to remind him of his place and also to make him more aware of my needs as a woman."

Jessica ended up taking most of her pasta home in a plastic container. Alyssa wondered about the propriety of a girl serving as a slave to her professor, but hoped the Domina training would help Jessica more than the enslavement harmed her.

Chapter Fourteen

"Lawrence won't send you to me so I can beat you anymore." Bryce had his arm wrapped around Jessica and she nestled her head against his shoulder. She found it ironic that after throwing her around and abusing her for hours at a time he always wanted to cuddle. Although she didn't feel the least bit affectionate toward him, especially after such rough sex, he paid her a great deal of money for her companionship, so she pretended that she enjoyed it.

"One of the new professors is a submissive. Professor Lawrence has trained me to Domme him. Can't exactly show up as someone's Mistress with my ass red from your paddle."

Bryce sucked in his breath. "Next time you come over I want you to wear your Domme outfit. Geeze, I would love to rape a FemDom."

"Only if you promise not to damage any of it." Jessica surveyed the remains of a nun's habit and priest's cassock costumes scattered across the bed. "That stuff's expensive."

"I promise if anything gets damaged, I'll pay to replace it." He rolled over on top of her and thrust his tongue into her mouth, humping her thigh with his erection.

When he released her mouth to move his lips down her neck to her breasts, Jessica said: "Just the thought of raping a Domme turns you on? Why?"

He lifted his head. "Ultimate fantasy. On my knees, at your mercy, then turning the tables. So hot." Prying her legs apart with his knees, he thrust himself inside her. He pounded into her so hard, her breasts shook and her head bounced on the pillow.

J

Three days later, Jessica arrived at Bryce's house wearing her short leather skirt, leather bustier, suspender hose, boots, and gloves. She hesitated before opening the door from the garage into the foyer. After two months of topping Tom, allowing Bryce to dominate her rankled. But the play rape scenes had less of a submissive feel than the behavior required by Professor Lawrence. And she could still use the money. Although she visited Tom twice a week, two hundred and forty dollars didn't make up for a thousand. She had started relaxing more about her finances, buying the occasional new outfit, enjoying restaurant and takeout meals more often, hiring someone to clean her apartment once a month. She didn't care to give any of that up.

Opening the door, she entered the house and went upstairs to find Bryce naked on his knees in his bedroom. When she stood in front of him, he kissed the tops of her boots. "Thank you, Mistress, for honoring me with your presence." Knowing he intended to attack her, his words didn't give her the same thrill that she got from Tom.

Jessica retrieved a dog collar and cuffs from where he had left them on the bed and buckled them around his neck, wrists, and ankles. She grabbed his hair, pulled him to his feet, and pushed him on his back onto the bed. Straddling him, she scooted up his torso and reached for his cuffs with links in hand to attach them to the bed posts. Bryce grabbed her wrists and flipped over so she lay on her back with him straddling her. Even though she knew he had planned to turn the tables, his assault still took her by surprise. Instinctively, she brought her knee up between his legs, punching him in the balls. When he doubled over, she pushed him off her and rolled out from under him and off the bed.

"How dare you attack your Mistress, you little worm." Bryce still gripped his crotch with both hands and whimpered in pain. Jessica took advantage of his position to clip his wrists to his ankles. "I'll punish you for such insolence."

Bryce gasped for breath. "You bitch. I never said you could kick me in the nuts. You're the only one who's getting punished for this."

Jessica's nostrils flared. She had accepted Bryce's abuse for almost a year and although he paid her well for the privilege, now she couldn't bear the thought of allowing him to force her to submit to him. She grabbed the paddle that had blistered her rear so many times from the top of the chest of drawers and swung it at his backside.

"Ow," he screamed. "How dare ... you little slut."

"The proper response is 'That's one, Mistress. Thank you, Mistress." She hit him again.

"Damn you. That hurts. Stop it or I'll report you to Lawrence."

"And admit you've been paying me to see you behind his back, taking money out of his pocket and fucking his collared slave?" Jessica swung the paddle again.

Bryce rolled to one side and she hit his hip instead of his ass. He screamed and she could see an ugly bruise forming over the bone.

For a moment, Jessica hesitated. This man had treated her better than any of the other faculty the Professor had forced her to submit to. Bryce's money had allowed her to purchase a car and enjoy some of the luxuries her father's death had forced her to forgo. "You shouldn't try to avoid your punishment, you'll only get hurt worse." With one hand holding his hip down, Jessica brought the paddle down hard on his buttocks again. She knew every blow further shredded their relationship, but she could no longer tolerate the thought of submitting to any man. The Professor might force her to suck his limp penis, but she promised herself, no one else would ever put her on her knees again.

She swung the paddle. Bryce had tears streaming down his face and his backside had taken on a bright red hue after only five strikes. "That would be five, boy."

"Yes, Mistress. Thank you, Mistress."

Panting, Jessica stopped in midstroke, one knee on the bed her other foot on the floor. The submission in Bryce's words relieved the anger his assault had triggered. She pushed herself away from the bed and returned the paddle to the chest. She sat down on the other side of the bed and pulled Bryce's head into her lap. "I'm sorry, Bryce, but you shouldn't have asked me to come over here as a Domme. I just can't make the transition when I'm dressed like this."

"You're one hell of a bitch, aren't you?" He looked up at her with an admiring look.

"Let's just say that dominating comes much more naturally to me than submitting does." She wiped his tears away with her thumb.

"If I let you tie me up, will you ride my cock?" He leered at her.

"I only allow my submissives to worship me orally and accept my strap-on in their ass." She grabbed a hunk of his hair and pulled his face up to within inches of hers. He tried to kiss her, but she stayed just out of reach.

"No strap-on, but you can sit on my face for as long as you'd like if you'll ride my cock until I come."

The thought of making Bryce pleasure her orally, after all the times he had come in her mouth, made Jessica wet. And if she kept him bound while she rode him, she could tease him unmercifully before she allowed him release. "Only if I can pinch and bite and you don't come until you ask for, and I give you, permission."

"Pinch and bite my nipples if you like. Nothing else."

Jessica unclipped his wrists from his ankles and dragged them toward the head of the bed. He let her clip the cuffs to the plastic chain he kept secured around the bed posts. She fastened his ankles to the posts at the foot of the bed. With a knee on either side of him, she worked her way up his legs and torso to his head. By the time she lowered herself over his face, she was panting. Having him at her mercy, unable to touch her, forced to pleasure her, made her dizzy with power.

Bryce obediently thrust his tongue up between her nether lips and lapped at her. Jessica moaned and pushed herself down further. Bryce responded by sucking on her clit until she grabbed the headboard to keep from falling over. Her tremors shook the entire bed. He moaned, but kept licking. Jessica made him bring her off half a dozen times and only stopped because her clit got so sensitive his tongue offered more stimulation than she could bear.

She slid back down his torso and stopped when she bumped into his erection. Leaning over, she grabbed one of his nipples with her teeth. At first he moaned, but she kept pressing into his flesh until he screamed. Then she bit the other one. Bryce struggled against the restraints binding him to the bed and Jessica laughed. She reached behind herself, grabbed him in her hand, and squeezed it until he cried out before raising herself high enough to guide him into her. Sex felt so much better, she decided, when she controlled how and where.

Throwing her head back, she rode him until she came

again. If he tried to move his hips, she leaned forward and pinched his nipples until he stayed still under her.

"Please, Mistress, may I come?" Bryce's eyes had rolled back in his head and she could feel his hips tightening.

Jessica pushed herself off him and grabbed a nipple in her teeth. "No," she said around it.

He screamed. She didn't know whether from pain or frustration, but she didn't care. When his body relaxed into the bed, Jessica mounted him again. Three times she stopped when he begged to come, reveling each time in the power he had ceded to her.

"Oh, god, please, Mistress. I'm begging you. I need to come so badly." His voice sounded pained and he had a tortured grimace on his face.

Close to another orgasm of her own, Jessica didn't want to stop this time. She kept moving until the force of her own orgasm made her collapse on his chest. "You may come now, boy."

With his hands and legs bound to the bed, and her head a weight on his chest, Bryce had a hard time moving enough to climax, but Jessica had no interest in aiding his release. He finally came with a roar and for a while Jessica stayed sprawled on his chest.

"You are one hot bitch of a Mistress, you know that, don't you?" Bryce's breathing had finally subsided to normal.

Jessica pushed herself off him and the bed and went into the bathroom to wash up. When she emerged, she stood looking at the man who had abused her for so long and from whom she had extracted a small amount of revenge. She turned toward the door.

"Hey, you can't leave me like this."

"Actually, yes, I can." Jessica paused with her hand on the bedroom door. If she released him he could turn the tables again and she wanted to walk away still in control. "I'm sure you'll figure out a way to extricate yourself. Goodbye, Bryce."

"Wait, please, don't go."

Jessica shut the door and headed toward the stairs.

"Jessica," he hollered from the bedroom. "Please don't leave me. I need you."

"But, I don't need you," Jessica said aloud half way down the stairs, even though she knew Bryce couldn't hear her. She picked up the envelope on the dining room table that contained her payment and let herself out. With the money from her visits to Tom, she wouldn't have to give up her car. She would learn to do without everything else.

Chapter Fifteen

Although the Professor no longer sent her to submit to his colleagues in their homes, he still required her to attend his parties. Tom never appeared and she didn't know if Professor Lawrence invited him or not. Taking off her clothes in front of the faculty members who enjoyed the Professor's hospitality and accepting the abuse he permitted became more difficult at each event. The Professor allowed no one to beat her or do anything else that left marks. But she still had men tying her up, coming in her mouth, pushing dildoes into her, and watching her make love to Sandra.

Professor Lawrence's annual holiday party gave her the opportunity to redeem her self-esteem, somewhat. He invited everyone on the University faculty, not just the men who paid for the privilege of abusing his slaves. Some of the staff and many more students than those who served him received coveted invitations to the event. Everyone wore clothing, the door to the dungeon stairs remained locked, and hired caterers prepared and served the food.

"You look stunning tonight, my dear," the Professor whispered in her ear when he greeted her at the door.

Jessica repressed the bile that his cologne always brought to her throat and stepped inside. She had splurged on a new outfit, although she had purchased it at Nordstrom's Rack, for the evening. She had found a black, silk, Carmen Marc

Valvo halter dress with a lace insert under the bust marked down to a hundred and twenty — one evening of putting Tom on his knees — from the original price of five hundred dollars. The dress emphasized her generous breasts and narrow waist and she looked good in black, she decided. Jessica had hung the key from the collar around her neck and wore dangly earrings made from similar, but smaller, links that she had also found at the Rack.

Although she appreciated someone noticing the effort she had put into her appearance, she would have preferred the compliment come from anyone but the Professor. She stood to one side and watched him welcome each guest — students, colleagues, and clients — who entered his home with a handshake or a hug.

Candles sparkled from the tables and the mantle and filled the air with scents of cinnamon and cloves. An eight-foot blue spruce, decorated with tiny white lights and red, green, and blue balls, added pine fragrance to the mix. Jessica turned away from the door and marveled at the bounty offered in the dining room. Trays of maki sushi, smoked salmon blini, coconut shrimp, mushrooms stuffed with crab, jerked chicken wings, brie, Camembert, Stilton, and bowls of caviar covered the huge table. She resisted the delicacies for the moment and wandered among the guests, greeting the faculty and staff she knew from school, avoiding the men she had met at the Professor's other parties. In the living room, punch bowls of eggnog, wassail, and fruit juices sat surrounded by glass cups on a table against the wall.

Uniformed staff poured the guests' beverage choices, replenished the trays, and removed plates and glasses. Before Jessica could request something to drink, she saw Tom balancing a cup of eggnog in one hand and a plate of canapes in the other talking to an instructor she had never seen before.

"Good evening, Professor Ross." Jessica walked up and

offered a hand to the woman standing in front of him. "Hi, I'm Jessica Richards. Are you both enjoying the party?"

The woman, a short, dumpy redhead, wearing a badly-fitting, off-the-rack green suit, gave Jessica a limp handshake. "I'm Roberta Howard. I teach English."

"Pleased to meet you. You're in the English Department also, aren't you, Professor Ross?"

Tom nodded and took a sip of his eggnog.

"Jessica." The Professor's voice carried over the myriad conversations scattered throughout the room and the muted carols playing on the stereo.

"Well, you two have a lovely evening." Jessica turned away and swung her hips gracefully, letting her full skirt swirl around her legs, as she strolled toward the Professor, who stood in front of the dining room table.

A tiny blonde stood at the Professor's elbow. "Jessica, this is Isadora Jameson. I'm trying to convince her to switch majors. I think she would make an amazing psychology student. Perhaps you'll have better luck." He walked away, striding toward a cluster of guests standing in front of the tree.

"Don't bother. I really don't have any intention of majoring in psychology. I took one of his graduate classes to satisfy an MFA requirement and he's hounded me ever since." Isadora's head barely came up to Jessica's shoulder, giving Jessica a lovely view of her ample breasts barely contained in the bodice of her strapless, royal blue taffeta dress.

"Don't worry, Isadora. I'm not in the habit of convincing people to change their majors." Jessica didn't care the least what subject Isadora studied, she only wanted to know the woman's sexual orientation.

"In that case, call me Dora." The woman's smile lit up her eyes so they sparkled like sapphires.

"If he's hounded you, why did you come to his party?" Jessica wanted more than anything else to pull down the blue bodice and sink her teeth into Dora's nipples.

Dora turned and swept a slender arm over the table. "Where else does a student get to eat like this?" She took one of the gold-rimmed china plates and piled morsels from the trays onto it.

Jessica took a plate for herself and cut off small wedges of Camembert and brie, selected one of the blini, a shrimp, and added a few water crackers and a spoonful of caviar. She followed Dora over to the punch bowls and accepted a cup of eggnog from the server. She looked around the room, but someone sat in every available seat. "Let's take these," Jessica lifted her plate slightly, "somewhere we can enjoy them in peace."

Dora smiled and Jessica wanted very much to kiss her. She led the woman to the Professor's study. Balancing the plate on her cup, she tapped on the door. When no one answered, she turned the handle and peered inside. Jessica pushed open the door, flipped on the light switch, and stood aside so Dora could enter. Closing the door behind her, she set plate and cup on the Professor's desk and seated herself in one of the leather wingback chairs pointing Dora to the other.

"You seem to know your way around the place." Dora nibbled on a shrimp with luscious lips.

"Professor Lawrence is my advisor." Jessica took a sip of eggnog and tasted a hefty spike of rum under the sweet, creamy, nutmeg flavor.

"I've heard he's hit on more than one of his female students." Dora licked off her fingers and edged a piece of maki out from under another shrimp and a blini. She tilted her head to one side, the seaweed-wrapped roll of rice and raw fish hovering near those delicious lips. "That true?"

Jessica shrugged. "If you're not his student, why do you care?" She took her plate from the desk, but none of the tidbits she'd selected had any appeal compared to the one that sat in the chair across from her.

"Because his classes are interesting and I'd like to take another. But not if I have to put up with harassment." Dora finished the maki and hesitated before selecting the blini to try next.

"Perhaps you should take classes from someone else then." Jessica set her plate back on the Professor's desk. "Although, you'll find many of the psychology professors are just as lecherous."

Dora popped the round buckwheat pancake topped with gravlax and a sprig of dill into her mouth and chewed.

Jessica thought how wonderful that mouth would feel between her legs. "What's your major?"

"Creative writing. I'm working on a novel for my thesis." Dora smiled and mischief lit her eyes. "My protagonist is a lesbian and my advisor is having hissy fits."

Jessica took Dora's plate and cup and set them on the desk. She reached over and ran her fingers through the girl's silky blond hair and then tightened her grip. With a fistful of hair, she pulled the blonde's face toward hers. Dora didn't resist and Jessica found her acceptance of the rough handling encouraging. Their lips met and Jessica thrust her tongue between Dora's, tasting the salty salmon and remnants of wasabi. Dora sucked eagerly on Jessica's tongue. Jessica yanked harder at the girl's hair and pulled her from her seat to her knees in front of the chair. Dora slipped her arms around Jessica's waist and Jessica let her free hand drift over the soft skin of Dora's neck, shoulders, and back.

Panting, Jessica released Dora and pushed herself back in her chair. "Did you drive here?"

Dora sat back on her heels. "No, Ma'am. I took the bus."

Jessica smiled. "You're a submissive?"

"Yes, Ma'am. I think that's why the professor hit on me. Only I'm also a lesbian, something I don't think he's figured out yet."

Jessica laughed, delighted to find out her suspicions about Dora's orientation were correct. She ran one finger down Dora's cheek. "We probably should get back to the party or someone's bound to come looking for us. I'll come find you when I'm ready to leave and drive you home."

"May I ask one question, first, Ma'am?"

"Yes."

"You wear a collar?"

Jessica sighed. She didn't want to confess her situation, but she couldn't expect Dora to submit to her willingly if she wasn't honest. "I needed Professor Lawrence to accept me as a student. He would only do so if I wore his collar. Right now, I switch, topping a submissive professor for him, and submitting to Professor Lawrence when I must. That will end as soon as I complete my dissertation."

"You're bisexual?"

Jessica rose to her feet. "You were given permission to ask one question. If you're still here when I'm ready to leave, I'll take you home. If not ..." She picked up her plate and cup and left the room. Dora had inadvertently touched a raw nerve. Although Jessica had enjoyed male lovers in the past, the Professor had created an association between sex and submission in her mind. She found herself unwilling to have any sexual interaction with men, although she still allowed Tom to worship her orally.

Rejoining the party, Jessica tried to socialize with the other students and faculty members she knew. But, time and again she found herself searching the room for Dora. Occasionally she spotted the other woman, usually cornered by one male or another. But often Dora seemed to disappear, convincing Jessica she'd left the party. When her hunger got the best of her, Jessica made a meal of shrimp and cheese, but she didn't really taste her food. She waited until several other guests had said their goodbyes and then retrieved her coat from the closet.

"Leaving so early." The Professor raised an eyebrow when she approached him to say goodnight.

"Sorry, Sir," she whispered. "I'm not feeling terribly well."

He leaned down and put his mouth close to her ear. "Did you make any progress with Isadora?"

She shook her head. "I'm afraid she's a lesbian, Sir."

The Professor snorted.

Chapter Sixteen

Jessica stepped out into the frigid Chicago winter and found Dora waiting for her on the Professor's front porch. She smiled, but didn't acknowledge the girl. Dora followed her down the stairs and stayed behind her until they reached the blue Mustang. Then she scurried ahead and opened the door. Jessica slid behind the wheel and fastened her seat belt while Dora walked around the car and climbed in.

Neither spoke during the drive to Jessica's apartment. Dora jumped out of the car as soon as Jessica pulled up the parking brake. By the time Jessica shut off the engine and turned off the lights, Dora had her door open. Her attitude made Jessica want to throw her against the car hood and ravish her. She took a deep breath, swung her long legs out of the car, and rose to her feet. After Dora closed the door, Jessica locked the car with the remote and walked through the underground garage towards the elevator with Dora following.

When they entered the apartment, Dora fell to her knees and kissed Jessica's feet. "Thank you so much, Ma'am, for allowing me this opportunity to serve you."

Jessica picked up one foot then the other, allowing Dora to reverently remove each shoe. The girl then stood and took off Jessica's coat. She hung that in the closet and set the shoes inside on the floor. "Shall I get undressed, Ma'am?"

"Yes." Jessica had never felt so at home in her own

apartment. She walked over to the sofa, sank into the supple leather, and watched Dora unzip the dress and let it slide off her voluptuous frame.

Underneath she wore only a blue lace garter belt, flesh-colored hose, and a satiny blue thong. After hanging the dress in the closet, Dora unfastened the garters and slowly rolled first one then the other stocking down her leg. Jessica realized her breathing had gotten heavier. When Dora had removed her shoes and hose, she slid the garter belt and thong down her hips and let them drop to the floor. She lifted them with her toe and plucked them off. Jessica wiggled in anticipation of getting her hands on Dora's delectable curves. The girl had large, plump breasts with small pink areola and firm little nipples pierced through with barbells. Her narrow waist flared out to ample hips. She had shaved her lovely thick labia and studs of a Christina piercing peeked out from the tops of her slit and pubic mound.

Dora knelt in front of Jessica and took one foot in both hands. With strong fingers, she massaged Jessica's stocking foot from the heel to the ball. Jessica sighed. Despite the frequency with which she was forced to wear them, she found her feet still ached at the end of an evening in stilettos. When Dora had relieved the pain in both of her feet, she took Jessica's big toe in her mouth and sucked on it. Jessica moaned with pleasure. Dora sucked and licked Jessica's feet until her stockings were wet with saliva.

Jessica lifted her skirt above her garters. "You may remove my stockings."

"Yes, Ma'am. Thank you, Ma'am." Dora undid the two garters on top and Jessica lifted her legs slightly off the sofa so Dora could get underneath and unfasten those. Jessica could almost feel sparks ignited by the touch of Dora's fingers. Dora used her teeth to pull Jessica's stockings off her leg, moving from back to front as needed, letting her lips caress Jessica's skin. When Jessica's legs were naked, Dora kissed the inside of her thighs. "Perhaps Ma'am would allow me the honor of giving her a massage. I have training in sensual techniques."

Jessica rose and walked toward the bedroom with Dora following on her hands and knees. After flipping on the bedside light, Jessica rummaged in the nightstand and extracted an old bottle of vanilla-scented massage oil. She turned her back to Dora who unhooked the top of her dress and pulled the zipper down with her teeth. Lifting the straps of the halter over Jessica's head, Dora sighed appreciatively when she brought it down to reveal Jessica's breasts. She licked her lips and Jessica could see the longing in her face. Dora's desire fueled her own.

When Dora had removed the garter belt, Jessica grabbed the girl by the hair and kissed her hard. Their breasts pressed together and Jessica reached back to grab Dora's lovely round backside in her hand. She pressed her nails into the girl's plump flesh and much to her delight, Dora moaned with pleasure. Jessica kissed her way down to Dora's breast and took her pierced nipple in her mouth. When she bit down, Dora stood on her tiptoes, pushing her breast tight against Jessica's mouth.

A submissive and a masochist. How delightful. Jessica stepped away from the girl and lay face-down on the bed, her head resting on her arms. Dora moved Jessica's hair above her shoulder, poured some of the massage oil into her palms and rubbed them together to warm it. She stroked Jessica's shoulders, back, and rear, rubbing in the oil and setting Jessica's skin on fire.

Everything Dora did seemed intended for Jessica's pleasure. Even though Jessica enjoyed putting Tom on his knees, she was always aware that her behavior satisfied the man's sexual need. For the first time, she experienced someone truly serving her and enjoying only the pleasure given. She found the experience intoxicating. Jessica rolled over on her back and allowed Dora to apply the oil to her breasts, tummy, legs and arms. When Jessica wriggled in frustration and need, Dora obediently brought her mouth down between Jessica's legs. Her tongue snaked out and slid between Jessica's nether lips.

Jessica gasped. Dora had a metal stud in her tongue. When that hit Jessica's clit, the pent-up tension exploded. Jessica grabbed Dora by the hair and pushed her face tighter between her legs. Dora licked, sucked, and used her stud to make Jessica come again and again. Finally Jessica dragged Dora's face up to her own and rolled over on top of her. Her mouth on one breast, her finger and thumb pinching the nipple on the other, Jessica brought her knee up between Dora's legs and pounded it against her until the girl shuddered in orgasm.

Rolling over on her back, Jessica wrapped her arms around Dora and the girl nestled her head against Jessica's shoulder. "Thank you, so much, Ma'am. That was just wonderful. I hope you were pleased."

Jessica stroked Dora's soft hair. "Very pleased, my dear. Very pleased." Jessica reached over and pulled the comforter over the two of them. "I think I want to keep you."

"Oh, thank you, Ma'am. I would like that very much. May I call you Mistress?" Dora snuggled closer.

Jessica smiled. That word had never sounded so good to her ears. She tightened her grip around Dora. "You may."

Although Dora drifted off to sleep immediately, Jessica found herself too bedazzled by the events of the evening to relax. She didn't know which turned her on more: Dora's consummate submission unadulterated by money or any other expected reward, or that the submission came from a woman. Tom's submission carried an expectation that in exchange for the money he gave the Professor, he would receive precisely what he asked for. Jessica had a list of torments he wanted her to inflict and activities he considered off limits. In truth, he had more control over their encounters than she did.

Dora, on the other hand, gave herself to Jessica unconditionally, offering her body to please her Mistress with no expectation of anything in return. And what an exquisite body, she had. Jessica ran a hand along Dora's back and caressed her lovely, firm curves. Jessica had never experienced the intensity of pleasure Dora had given her. Even her encounters with Sandra, although more pleasurable than any other experience she had since accepting the Professor's collar, didn't compare.

She stroked Dora's hair and the girl murmured in her sleep. Realistically, they had just met. She couldn't expect Dora to accept her collar, nor, Jessica realized, was she prepared to offer it so soon. But, Jessica hoped that they could work toward that. She wanted to go to sleep every night with this woman in her arms and wake up to find her there as well.

J

Jessica awoke in an empty bed. She frowned, but then realized she smelled coffee brewing. She got up and headed for the bathroom. When she emerged, she found Dora kneeling by the bed, a tray laden with a pot of hot coffee, mug, creamer, sugar bowl, butter dish, all three kinds of jam from the fridge and a plate of toast on the nightstand.

"Mistress, I'm sorry I could only find bread, no eggs or flour to make pancakes or french toast. And I didn't know how you preferred your coffee so I brought the cream and sugar, but didn't put either in the cup. Perhaps you'll allow me to go shopping for you so I can prepare a proper breakfast for you tomorrow."

Jessica could think of nothing more delightful. She stopped to kiss Dora on the top of her head before climbing back into bed. "Toast is fine for this morning. I like my coffee with about a tablespoon of cream and two teaspoons of sugar."

Dora poured coffee into the cup and stirred in the proper amounts of cream and sugar. She handed the cup to Jessica and lifted a piece of toast. "Butter, Mistress?"

"Just marmalade." Jessica took a sip of the coffee. Home brew had never tasted quite this good. With Dora making her coffee, she would never miss lattes.

"May, I take a shower, now, Mistress? I don't want to be late for class."

While Dora filled the bathroom with steam, Jessica rummaged in her sweater drawer and found an oversized one that would fit over Dora's lovely breasts. She selected one of her shortest skirts and even then it came to Dora's knees. Since Dora only wore a size six, Jessica couldn't lend her any shoes. On the other hand, she liked the look of the girl's slender legs in stockings and high heels.

"What time do you get through with school?" Jessica stood by the front door of her apartment, Dora on her knees in front of her.

"I have class until three-thirty and I work at the Powell's on Lincoln until nine." Dora leaned over and planted a kiss on each of Jessica's feet. "Thank you so much for allowing me to serve you, Mistress. May I come here after work?"

"Do you have a car?"

"No, Mistress. I can take the bus."

"I'd rather you didn't, that late. I'll pick you up and we can go out for a late supper."

Dora looked up with a big smile. "Oh, thank you, Mistress. If you'd like, we can go back to my apartment and I can make something. I have plenty of food."

Jessica laughed. That didn't surprise her. "That sounds like an excellent idea. I'll see you at nine."

Dora kissed her feet again. Jessica lifted Dora's head up by her hair and pressed her lips against Dora's. She thrust her tongue into the girl's mouth for a moment before releasing her.

After Dora left, Jessica showered, enjoying the smell of another woman in her bathroom. She spent the day writing her dissertation, eager to get as much of her work done so she could enjoy her evening with Dora.

Chapter Seventeen

"I have a confession to make." Jessica stroked Dora's back, enjoying the feel of red welts under her fingers. She ran her fingernails over the skin abrasions and Dora moaned.

"Yes, Mistress." Dora kissed Jessica's fingers when, while caressing her shoulders, they strayed close to her mouth.

"I've submitted to more than just Professor Lawrence. He has a dungeon in his basement and he hosts parties for other professors who are sadists. He forces his collared slaves to accept abuse at the parties and he also sends them out to serve the professors in their homes."

"They say the best Dommes always bottom first." Dora rolled over on her side and lowered her head to Jessica's breast. She lapped at the nipple with her tongue and teased it erect.

Jessica sighed with pleasure and relief. For weeks she had worried about Dora's reaction to her servitude, but felt compelled to tell her the unvarnished truth. "For several months, I saw one of the other professor's behind Professor Lawrence's back. I only did it because he paid me quite well for the privilege of raping me in various get-ups. I stopped seeing him when the professor trained me to Domme his submissive colleague."

Dora moved her head to give the other breast her attention. "And, Mistress is telling me this, why?"

Although Dora still had her apartment, she spent almost

no time there. Most of her clothing had found space in Jessica's closets. Dora did all the shopping, cooking, cleaning, and laundry. Jessica chose the girl's clothing, told her what she could eat, and monitored her schedule. But, Jessica found herself needing even more. She wanted Dora dependent on her, emotionally and financially. Jessica needed Dora to have nowhere else to go.

"Because I want to collar you and you need to know what I've done to get to this point."

Dora gasped and released Jessica's nipple. She lifted her head and tears glistened in her eyes. "Oh, Mistress," she whispered. "Thank you so very, very much. I want so badly to wear your collar, to give myself to you for always."

Jessica smiled. She pulled Dora closer and kissed her mouth. The gentle touch turned passionate, and their lips locked together. She rolled Dora over on her back, crushing their breasts together, reveling in the younger woman's submission and acceptance.

J

Alyssa watched Jessica walk into the Chicago Chop House with a bounce to her step that left no doubt that their meal would be celebratory. Alyssa stood and embraced Jessica who wore a soft cashmere dress. "You positively radiate success, my dear."

"I present my findings on Anxiety Disorders in Patients Who Have Experienced Post Traumatic Stress at the University symposium next month."

"How wonderful. Things have come together nicely for you, my dear, haven't they." Alyssa returned to the ladder-backed chair at the table covered with crisp white linen. "I'm so very pleased. First, you met that lovely Dora. Now, you've finished your dissertation. What next?"

"I'll finish my internship and do my post-doctoral work at the University Mental Health Clinic. I can continue my research while getting enough experience treating patients to open my own practice in nine months or less." Jessica picked up the wine list. "The position carries a lot of prestige that I can leverage when I'm ready to go out on my own. I couldn't have gotten it without Professor Lawrence's support.

"May I get you ladies something to drink?" A dark-haired boy wearing a black vest over a white shirt with narrow tie stood at their table, hands behind his back.

"We'll have a bottle of the Taittinger Brut." Jessica handed him the wine list. "We're celebrating."

"I'll be right back with that."

"This one's on me." Jessica picked up the menu. "By this time next month, I'll be earning a real salary."

"And will you give up that, then?" Alyssa pointed to the collar hanging around Jessica's neck.

She sighed. "I'd like to. But as long as I stay affiliated with the University, he has a lot of influence over my career."

Alyssa took up her own menu. "If your Professor values your work for him as a Dominant, perhaps you can convince him to release you from servitude."

Jessica smiled. "Yes, I now have two professors at my feet. Apparently, Tom had a friend on the faculty who's also a submissive and he let him know of my," she licked her lips, "talents."

Alyssa laughed appreciating both the way Jessica's eyes lit up and remembering how much she had enjoyed her discovery that some men actually liked to have a woman hurt them.

"Tom sent Roger Smythe to Professor Lawrence last month. Unfortunately, Roger isn't near as much fun to Dominate as Tom." Jessica took a sip of water and wrinkled her nose. "He's forty pounds overweight and bald." She leaned across the table. "I don't allow him to worship me orally — I can barely tolerate him kissing my boots."

Alyssa shrugged. She remembered only too well how disappointing she found the appearance of many of the men who had wanted to hire her. "The price of professional Domination. Now you understand why I gave it up. What do you do with him, my dear?"

"Mostly I forced him to wear women's clothing and verbally abuse him." Jessica pressed her lips together. "Occasionally I'll take him over my knee and spank him."

"Does this satisfy him?"

"He keeps paying Professor Lawrence for me to come back."

The waiter returned and popped open their bottle, pouring the bubbly liquid into flute glasses. Alyssa took a sniff enjoying the frothy aroma of green apple and wheat. The bubbles tickling her nose, she sipped at the fresh, creamy flavors of apple and toasted bread.

"I'll have the ten-ounce filet with mashed potatoes." Jessica gave the boy her menu.

"And what kind of dressing would you like on your salad?"

"Creamy blue cheese."

The boy turned to Alyssa.

"The catfish almondine. Creamy garlic dressing."

"Thank you, ladies. I'll be right back with your salads."

"So what will you do tonight to celebrate?" Alyssa pulled off her reading glasses, stuck them in their metal case, and put it into her purse. Jessica seemed content to change the subject and Alyssa preferred not to dwell on thoughts of her brief pro career.

Jessica lifted her glass. "I think this will do nicely."

Alyssa clinked her glass against Jessica's. "Come, dear, you can't consider lunch, even at the Chop House, an adequate celebration. You've worked on your dissertation for what, two years now?"

Jessica shrugged. "Two years and forty days, actually. Not that I'm counting."

Alyssa glanced around to make sure no one could overhear her. "Why don't you come with me to Lady Gina's party tonight. FemDoms only, no male Tops."

Jessica grinned. "Really?"

"Usually she invites enough single males so we're outnumbered two or three to one. Any male who isn't owned must offer himself up as a community play toy." Alyssa smiled. Although in her younger days she had attended many parties, now she limited herself to those Lady Gina gave. She had found that she enjoyed public play much more without all the testosterone the male Doms threw about.

Jessica's grin got wide enough to show white teeth between her bright red lips.

"You can bring Dora, if you'd like, but there'll be lots of other toys to play with as well." Alyssa took another sip of the delicious champagne, enjoying Jessica's reaction.

"Oh, I'll bring Dora. If I have as much fun as you're implying, I'll need someone to," Jessica winked, "relieve the tension; something I'm not going to want from a boy I just met."

"Of course, dear, that's why I always bring Klark." That and she found it so much easier to play if she had him to clean up the station and pack up her toys while she gave aftercare to whatever boy she had played with.

The waiter sat plates of salad in front of them and proffered the pepper grinder. Jessica declined, but Alyssa had him grind some on hers.

When the waiter left them, Jessica leaned forward. "Tell me more about this party."

Alyssa lifted a fork full of dressing-drenched salad to her lips and made Jessica wait until she swallowed the garlicky lettuce. "Lady Gina has a rather large dungeon in her basement. Every other month, she invites a dozen or so of her FemDom friends. We're welcome to bring our submissives, and can invite one other FemDom if we know her personally." Alyssa would need to call Gina as soon as she returned home and let her know she would bring a guest. Gina did not like surprises and Alyssa didn't blame her.

Alyssa took a sip of water and reached for a roll. She needed something to cut the garlic. "What better way to celebrate completing your degree than with a flogger in your hand and a helpless male bound in front of you?"

Jessica swallowed her bite of salad and reached for her champagne. "Can't think of any." She dabbed her napkin to her lips, leaving a red stain on the white cloth.

When the waiter cleared their salad plates, Alyssa reached into her purse and pulled out a small package wrapped in gold paper with a black bow. "Happy graduation, dear." She pushed it across the table.

Jessica blinked her eyes rapidly for a moment, her lips parted slightly. "Alyssa, how sweet. You didn't have to get me a present."

"Of course, I didn't, dear. I wanted to." Alyssa had purchased it months ago and waited for the appropriate time to gift Jessica with it.

Jessica removed the bow and sliced through the tape with her fingernail. She removed the paper intact, opened the brown, clamshell box, and laughed. "How appropriate." She lifted the gold signet ring from the felt lining and tried to put it on the ring finger of her left hand. It slipped about so she moved it to the middle finger where it stayed in place nicely.

"Thanks so much, Alyssa." Jessica got up from her seat and came around the table to give Alyssa a hug. "I love it. And the party sounds wonderful. What time?"

"The party's up in Lake Forest. We'll pick you up at your apartment at eight."

The waiter set a piece of fish covered in almonds in front of Alyssa and she couldn't help wondering how he would look, bound to a cross, his naked back available for her whip. She smiled when he walked away from them; he did have a lovely rear.

Chapter Eighteen

L ady Gina lived in a stately mansion about forty-five minutes north of Chicago. Jessica smiled when a naked boy answered the front door and hung up their coats in the closet. Although she enjoyed watching women's bodies more than men's, the concept of a party allowing only submissive males provided a very welcome turnabout from the Professor's gatherings.

Klark and Dora stripped down to leather thongs. For a man his age, Klark had a surprisingly nice physique, Jessica thought as she followed Alyssa through a hallway to stairs leading down to the basement. About twice as big as Professor Lawrence's, the dungeon had a softer feel. Plush carpet covered the floor and the walls had wood paneling. Although Lady Gina had similar furniture, the room also had several sofas and other comfortable places to sit when not playing. And, Jessica reminded herself, no one would ever bind her to any of the equipment in this dungeon.

A dozen naked men and four almost-naked women had three- by five-inch paper tags attached to their collars. Jessica hesitated before selecting a cute, slender, red-headed boy who had CBT listed on his tag. She clipped a leash to the dog collar around his neck and led him over to an empty padded table. Dora followed with Jessica's leather duffle that now contained toys she had purchased for herself.

Jessica patted the table and the boy lay down on his back.

Dora handed her leather cuffs and Jessica fastened them around the boy's wrists and ankles and clipped those to hooks on the sides of the table. The power of taking control of a stranger to whom she had not spoken a word sent a rush to her head. Jessica ran her hands up and down the boy's chest, enjoying the firm muscles of youth. Although he kept himself in good shape, Tom probably had thirty years on this boy.

After pulling on a pair of exam gloves, Jessica ran one finger along the side of the boy's penis and it sprang to attention. He had almost eight inches and she grinned in anticipation of hurting it. Dora pulled a smaller, black leather case out from inside the duffle and handed it to Jessica.

After covering the boy's scrotum with clothespins, Jessica extracted her Wartenberg wheel. She held it in front of the boy's eyes and spun it with her finger, careful not to pierce the glove. He cringed and she laughed. Jessica started at his nipple which elicited a pained groan. She guided the wheel down the boy's chest, across his belly and up his erection. When the pins pricked the swollen head, he cried out. Jessica drew the wheel all around the head, then took it around the ridge at the bottom of his glans. He continued to holler, but he took a great deal more of the wheel than Tom could tolerate and Jessica enjoyed every minute of his pain.

She leaned over and whispered in his ear. "Shut up, boy. No one gave you permission to make so much noise." This boy hadn't paid her money to dominate him and she would require him to behave to her satisfaction.

"Yes, Ma'am. Sorry, Ma'am." The boy pressed his lips together.

Jessica smiled at his obedience and removed a six-inch vinyl flogger from the leather pouch. She held the boy's glans with one gloved hand and whipped the shaft, alternating between the top and the bottom. The boy squirmed in his bindings, but he kept quiet. She swiped the flogger at the clothespins that bristled from his scrotum. He made a strangled noise in his throat and she could see tears forming at the edge of his eyes. "Had enough, boy?"

"No, Ma'am. Thank you, Ma'am." The boy's voice had taken on a higher pitch, but he remained rock hard. Jessica so enjoyed playing with such a lovely toy. Although he claimed to like CBT, Tom usually lost his erection if Jessica used anything but pressure to inflict pain. Clothespins, the wheel, the flogger all made him go flaccid. She very much preferred playing with a hard toy than a soft one.

Jessica tortured the boy until, when she asked if he'd had enough, he acquiesced. Then she unclipped him from the table, sat him up, climbed up next to him, and took him in her arms. The boy trembled and Dora brought him a blanket. He clung to Jessica's waist and buried his face in her cleavage. She stroked his thick hair that covered his entire head and enjoyed the firm young body in her embrace.

Dora brought him a bottle of water from a cooler near the dungeon entrance and he gulped it down. When the boy's breathing returned to normal, Jessica pulled off her gloves, removed the cuffs from his wrists and ankles, and led him over to one of the sofas. She unclipped her leash and his tag from his collar and handed him the tag. Planting a kiss on the top of his forehead, she told Dora to keep on eye on him and went in search of another victim. She saw no reason not to take advantage of all these pretty young boy toys to play with, such a refreshing change from Tom's aging body.

Eight women wearing everything from leather corsets to latex body suits abused boys and girls bound to crosses, locked in cages, and strapped on medical tables. The sound of leather singing through the air, wood slapping against flesh, and screams of pain filled the room. The scent of sweat, arousal, and the all-pervasive smell of leather permeated the air. The excitement of knowing that she could play with any male in the room appealed to Jessica so much after all the parties she had attended in the Professor's dungeon.

A few women sat on the sofas or in the chairs providing aftercare to submissives they had played with. At least a dozen boys and girls wandered around longingly watching others play. After reading tags on several boys, Jessica found a cute youngster who listed singletail. She claimed him and found an empty cross. When she had the boy bound securely, she pulled out her four-foot signal whip. Standing back, she caressed the boy's backside with the leather, swinging it lightly back and forth.

She stepped closer and gradually increased the weight of the strokes she applied, slowing down as she did so. For a moment she paused and ran her hand across his very pretty rear. "Ready for me to hit you for real?"

He shuddered. "Yes, Ma'am. Thank you, Ma'am."

Jessica stepped back and swung the whip hard enough to raise a welt. The boy stood up on his toes and she waited until he brought his heels down before she swung again. She crisscrossed his back with angry red stripes, enjoying the sound of the whip striking flesh, the smell of the leather in her hand, the way the boy clenched and unclenched his fists when she hit him. Mostly she enjoyed watching his chiseled muscles cringe in anticipation of her stroke and the fact that she got to decide if and for how long she played with him. Sometimes she would step back and swing the whip so that it barely grazed his skin just to watch his reaction.

By the time she took him down from the cross, he winced when she touched him anywhere on his back. With a shoulder under his arm, she helped him stumble over to a sofa. She let him lay on his side with his head on her lap while she played with his hair until he pushed himself upright.

"Thank you so much, Ma'am." He pressed his lips together. "If I may say so, you smell divine. I was wondering if you would permit me to taste you. I've been told I'm very good with my tongue."

Jessica planted a kiss on the middle of his forehead. "Not tonight, boy. Perhaps another time." He couldn't hide the look of disappointment on his face, but he knelt, kissed her feet, and left her sitting on the sofa. As much as she had enjoyed hurting the boy, Jessica had no desire to get intimate with him. She only wanted one face between her legs. She snapped her fingers at Dora who immediately knelt in front of her. Jessica pointed at her crotch and Dora smiled before lifting the flared black skirt of the Valvo halter dress just enough to put her head underneath.

Dora kissed her way up the inside of Jessica's thigh and nuzzled aside her thong with her nose. After abusing two boys for almost an hour each, the inside of Jessica's thighs had gotten sticky. It only took a few hits from Dora's studded tongue to make Jessica come. Acutely aware of the other women around her, Jessica clamped down on the cry that tried to escape her lips. She tugged on Dora's hair and pulled the girl's face out from under her skirt after only one orgasm. "You can have more of that to enjoy when we get home."

Dora smiled and licked her lips. "Yes, Mistress. Thank you, Mistress."

Alyssa walked over to the sofa, Klark following on his hands and knees. "Have you enjoyed yourself, my dear?"

"Immensely."

"I hope you don't mind leaving now, then. I'm a bit tired."

Jessica looked at her watch. "No wonder, it's after midnight."

After saying goodbye to their hostess, the four climbed into Alyssa's baby blue Prius. Klark guided the car through the dark streets. Dora leaned her head against Jessica's shoulder and Jessica absent-mindedly twirled strands of Dora's blonde hair with her fingers. She thought how much she had enjoyed playing with the boys at the party where other women could see her skills at CBT and the way she could handle a single tail. The idea that one of those woman might have seen Jessica bound to a cross herself, or with her breasts punctured by needles, disgusted her. She had to wonder if any of them had recognized the collar around her neck despite her attempt to disguise it with a key.

Jessica caressed Dora's face and let her hand drift down her slave's neck to the gold chain that encircled it. Dora had given herself to Jessica, even knowing her history with the Professor. But an owner couldn't have a Master.

"Alyssa, would you mind if we stopped at an all-night hardware store?"

"What do you need, dear?" Alyssa turned and peered into the back seat.

"A pair of bolt cutters." Jessica fingered the collar around her neck.

"I have a pair in the back. I enjoy using chains and I keep the bolt cutters handy for safety. What do you need them for?"

"Can we stop by Professor Lawrence's house?"

"That would please me immensely." Alyssa turned back to face the windshield, but Jessica could see her broad smile reflected in the glass..

Twenty minutes later, Jessica stood on the Professor's porch, gripping the bolt cutters so tightly her hand started to cramp. Felicia opened the door and told her she could find the Professor in the dungeon. Jessica took a deep breath and walked down the steps without removing her coat.

Half a dozen men played with girls bound to crosses, tied onto padded tables, or strapped to the dental chair. The Professor stood, a cane in his hand and Sandra, suspended from the ceiling, swinging in front of him.

Jessica walked up to him and grabbed the ropes so that Sandra hung motionless.

"What do you think you're doing, slave?" The Professor's nostrils flared and his voice shook.

"I am not your slave any longer." Jessica kept her voice

low to avoid alerting the others in the dungeon, deeply involved in their own scenes, to her defiance. Although she wanted freedom from the Professor, she still needed his endorsement and saw no reason to embarrass him in front of his clientele.

She ignored his indignant sputtering and lifted the bolt cutters to her neck, captured a link, and pressed the handle together with all her strength until it snapped. The chain slid to the cement floor with a clatter. She lifted up her left hand. "I am a Dominant. I will never sub to you or any of your cronies again."

Turning on her heel, she strode out of the dungeon and up the stairs. She would have liked to have seen the expression on her former Master's face, but she opted for a dramatic exit instead. Letting herself out, she walked to the car idling at the curb and returned the bolt cutters to the box in the back. When she climbed inside and fastened her seat belt, Dora leaned over and kissed her at the base of her now bare neck.

"Well done, my dear." Alyssa turned to smile at Jessica while Klark eased the car back onto the road. "You've made me very proud of you. You've completed your dissertation, I was impressed with the way you played with the boys at the party, and now you've reclaimed your dignity. Quite a day, quite a day."

Jessica pulled Dora into her arms. The girl slid one hand up the inside of Jessica's thigh and tickled her nether lips with a finger. Jessica pushed her thighs apart a little to give Dora better access.

"Should we stop for a nightcap to celebrate?" Alyssa faced the front of the car again and couldn't see what Dora was up to.

"Thanks, but it is pretty late and after all the excitement, I'm rather tired." Jessica managed to control her breathing enough to get the words out, but Dora had found her clit and Jessica had to take slow, deep breaths.

J

"That little display the other night was quite uncalled for." Professor Lawrence sat behind the desk in his office at the University, scowling.

"I wonder what the chancellor would think of a professor who enslaves his students and pimps them out to other members of the faculty." Jessica crossed one leg over the other. She had deliberately worn jeans and a bulky sweater.

The Professor's smile reminded her of a lion confronting a wounded zebra. "And what proof do you have of that, my dear. No one will back you up and without collaborating witnesses, it's just your word against mine. Which do you think will carry more weight with the chancellor?"

Jessica kept her expression as blank as she could, masking her anger.

"Fortunately, you have taken excellent care of Professors Ross and Smythe. They both appreciate your talents and demonstrate it quite generously. I also have learned that another professor might like to spend some time at your feet." He cleared his throat. "So, I've decided to forgive you that little outburst. I will not require you to wear my collar, nor will I compel you to serve in any other capacity." He lowered his voice. "But you will continue to visit these gentleman as often as they require."

"Only if you pay me more." Jessica resisted gripping the arms of her chair or any other movement that would alert the Professor to her nervousness. "I want sixty percent of what they pay you. After all, I'm the one doing all the work."

"You have a lot of nerve, slave. Remember where you would be if I hadn't taken you on as my student. You probably still wouldn't have completed your dissertation."

"Perhaps." Jessica swallowed. "But, I'm no longer a

student. After my post-doctoral work at the clinic, I intend to start my own practice and you'll no longer have any hold over me at all."

"Do you really think so?" The Professor sneered, a look that sent a chill down Jessica's spine. "Who do you think will refer patients to you if you don't have a reference to offer from your advisor? Where will you get the money to open an office? No, dear, my hold over you will never end.

He folded his hands together on his desk blotter. "However, since I would rather not train another slave to dominate these men, I'll pay you forty percent — twice what you're getting now. And you can continue to use my name as a reference to facilitate your advancement."

Jessica allowed a bit of a smile to flit across her face. Assuming each professor wanted to see her once weekly, that would give her four hundred and eighty dollars, plus her salary from the clinic, to live on. She could look for a bigger place, perhaps even a house with room in the basement for a dungeon. She hadn't expected the Professor to meet her halfway, and the fact that he did so seemed almost as much of a victory as the extra money.

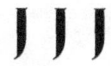

Acknowledgments

Many thanks to those all those who have contributed to my success by sharing their knowledge, skills, and support, including: boy robin, who served me well while he was under my protection; brad, who had more influence than he'll ever understand; Conrad Hodson; david; James; Deborah Dixon; and all the friends who encouraged me to persevere.

Other novels by Korin L. Dushayl include:

Shattered
Just where do you cross the point of no return?

When a sweet, intelligent twenty-five year old with un-diagnosed Asperser and PTSD seeks help from a ruthless, unscrupulous, sadistic therapist, she shatters his psyche and throws him into a suicidal depression. Her crude attempt to pick up the pieces -- enslaving him and subjecting him to un-ethical, unsanctioned, experiments -- ignores the lines of con-sent and the responsibilities of a Dominant. Just where does one cross the point of no return? -- Inspired by a true story.

"The work ... unfolds with the assured touch of a bestsell-ing mainstream author, seducing us into the lives of people with needs and agendas that find wings in the dark. Only an author familiar with this landscape could peel back these lay-ers of psychological complexity without flinching and with-out dramatic compromise ... Prepare to submit to this reading experience, which will mark you with its narrative power.
Larry Brooks, USA Today bestselling author of
Darkness Bound and *Bait and Switch*
(Read the first few pages starting on page 153)

Playing With Dolls
"a must read for anyone who ever had

to learn how to be comfortable in their own skin"
Jesse enjoys playing with dolls and wearing girls' clothing and everyone from his parents, teachers, friends and neighbors assumes he will grow up gay. As an adult the burden of those assumptions hampers his ability to come to terms with his sexuality"

Korin I. Dushayl "has done a great job depicting a young man's journey in discovering his true self."

Allena Gabosch, Executive Director
Center for Sex Positive Culture

"How one is labeled versus how one experientially comes to self-identification held a captivating tension for me. ... the everyday details in the story created a realistically immersive landscape that made it easier to viscerally identify with the characters."

Mark Silver

Korin I. Dushayl "has accomplished something remarkable here, crafting a story that works on all levels — educating, arousing, inspiring, empowering, and (most importantly) emotionally connecting with the reader."

Sally Bibrary, Bending the Bookshelf

Buy it in Print

or
E-Book

Choices
Must Linda's sexual awakening destroy her marriage?

From fairy tales to modern legal tradition, society demands we love exclusively, even though many only find happiness with multiple partners. Linda finally confronts long neglected sexual needs when Phil forces himself on her in Chicago. But back in Portland, her husband's insistence on monogamy compels her to choose between his limitations and her own insatiable desires.

But it in print

or E-Book

For more information visit
http://transgressivewriter.com

Chapter One

Zachary Smith lined all the brochure holders up with each other on the counter next to the window that protected the receptionist from the patients. Then, he straightened each stack of brochures in each holder. He rearranged the magazines on the oak coffee table, putting them in date order and set them on top of each the other so just the title of the magazine appeared beneath the magazine on top of it. He lined up the oak arm chairs so they each stood one inch away from the wall. As he reached out to straighten the metal-framed print of a still life with fruit and flowers that hung over the chairs, the receptionist's window slid open. "Mr. Smith, could you please sit down. Dr. Richards will be with you shortly, but you did arrive almost a half hour before your appointment." The frumpy woman wearing a dress covered in tiny white daisies stared at Zachary until he sat down. As soon as she closed the window again, he rose to his feet and fixed the picture. He stared at the clock over the window and watched the black second hand tick its way around the white face inside the white plastic frame.

The door next to the window opened and a beautiful woman, almost as tall as he, stepped out with a clipboard in her elegantly manicured hands. Slender, he guessed she couldn't weigh more than a hundred and twenty-five pounds, she had hair blacker than night that hung down and brushed her shoulders. She wore a tailored blue suit with a white blouse.

"Mr. Smith?"

Zachary looked up into her piercing green eyes and nodded.

"I'm Dr. Jessica Richards." She extended a hand and Zachary just stared at it, unwilling to sully such beauty, even if she permitted it. Eventually she withdrew it. "Why don't you come into my office, Mr. Smith."

Zachary followed the woman down a hallway of closed doors. She walked into one near the end and pointed to two upholstered armchairs under the window. Between them, a small metal table held a box of tissues, a water pitcher, and two glasses upside down on a tray. To get to a chair, he had to pass an oak desk which had a laptop computer, a pile of file folders, and a chrome lamp on it. Another chair, this one with wheels and levers to adjust the back and seat, sat in front of the desk.

Sitting in an armchair, Zachary put his hands in his lap. Then he put them next to his thighs. Then he sat on them.

"Let me just confirm some basic information, if I can." Dr. Richards held the top sheet off the clipboard and read from the page underneath. "You're twenty-five years old, you dropped out of the university in the middle of last term, and you live in Humboldt Park."

Zachary nodded.

"And why are you here at the clinic?" Zachary moved his hands between his thighs. "Zachary, or do you prefer Zach?" "Zachary," he whispered. "Ummm, could I see someone else?" How could he explain what he needed to this beautiful woman? He had never had a female therapist before, never mind one so stunning.

"Perhaps, you could give me a chance first?" Dr. Richards turned over one of the glasses and filled it half full of water from the pitcher. "We've only just met."

She pushed the glass toward Zachary; he took it and emptied it in one swallow.

"According to the forms you filled out, you have problems with anxiety and depression, you don't do well in social situations, and all this has resulted in your dropping out of college where you majored in philosophy for the past three years. Is that correct?"

Zachary nodded. He wanted nothing more than to escape the confines of her office. He felt as if the room had gotten smaller since he sat down.

"Also, according to this, you've never held a job for longer than six weeks."

Zachary lowered his eyes and moved his hands back to his lap, clutching them together.

"Zachary, would you be more comfortable if I stood behind you while we talked?"

Zachary nodded his head. Maybe if he didn't have to look at her, he could explain his problems.

Z

When he left the clinic, Zachary tried to decide where to go. Already late for work, he didn't know if he should rush to get to the grocery store or just give it up and go home. If Ramona had the shift, she would just let him stay late to make up for the time. As long as he got all the shelves stocked and the expired dairy products out of the coolers, she didn't care too much about when he showed up. But Stella had already given him two warnings and had told him one more late arrival and she would ask Mr. Larson to fire him.

The bus pulling up to the stop in front of campus as Zachary approached would take him to the Treasure Island. He decided to go to work and hope for the best.

"Zachary," Ramona called when he pushed open the swinging door to the back room. "Don't punch in." She grabbed his arm and pulled him behind a stack of empty milk crates. "Stella's complained to Mr. Larson and you're on report. I'll fill out your timecard when you're done with your shift and you can tell him you forgot to punch in. Go ahead and take care of the dairy case. The pallets can wait until the store clears out a little, after the evening rush."

Zachary put on his apron, tied it around his waist, and grabbed one of the empty milk crates. He spent an hour pulling products that had passed their sell-by dates, replacing them with fresher items, and straightening the rows of milk cartons, cottage cheese containers, and butter boxes. He probably should call the clinic and tell them he wouldn't return for the appointment the frumpy receptionist had scheduled for him on Thursday. Dr. Richards seemed nice enough, but she asked so many questions he didn't know how to answer.

Z

Jessica ushered Zachary into her office for the third time. This one puzzled her. Usually she could diagnose a patient's primary and secondary issues by the end of the first visit. Although she thought she had determined Zachary's primary diagnosis, something beyond that had impacted his mental health but she could not determine what. She wondered if she might use him to test the intriguing research trickling out of Siberia.

"I have some information for you today that might prove useful." Jessica crossed her legs and folded her hands together. She still couldn't get Zachary to look at her. "Have you ever heard of Asperger's Syndrome?"

He shook his head.

"It's a very mild form of autism, and I believe that's why you have difficulty succeeding in social environments." Jessica hadn't known that much about it herself until she started comparing the behaviors commonly found among patients with Zachary's symptoms. Jessica handed him a brochure and read the paragraph she had circled in her copy. "Typically those who suffer from Asperger's are deficient in social skills, have difficulty with transitions or changes, develop obsessive routines, are preoccupied with particular subjects of interest, cannot read nonverbal cues such as facial expressions, tone of voice, and body language, and are overly sensitive to sounds, tastes, smells, and sights. Often, like yourself, they are extremely intelligent, but they don't always find productive ways to demonstrate that intelligence."

Zachary clutched his copy of the brochure, nodding at each point Jessica brought up. "Can I get a prescription then?"

"I'm afraid it's not that simple. No drug therapy is available for AS itself, although we can try medication to help with your depression and anxiety problems."

He frowned and crumpled the brochure in his hands. "Doesn't help anything to put a name on it, then."

"I disagree. If we work together we can help you develop the social skills you need to function in most environments. I think you can even reach a point where you could have some semblance of a normal life. However, most patients with Asperger's don't experience your level of social dysfunction. I believe very strongly that something else is causing your depression and anxiety and until we know what that is, I can't really design an effective treatment program."

Zachary scowled. In the three hours she had spent with him, he had hadn't smiled once. His expressions ranged from inscrutable to downright angry.

Chapter Two

Jessica met Zachary at the front door of the building and ushered him upstairs to her office. She had closed his official file, claiming that he had stopped keeping his appointments, and only saw him after the other interns and supervisors left for the evening. Her supervisor would never approve of using a patient to test out Speransky's therapy methods, but Jessica thought Zachary might be the perfect candidate.

Sitting at her desk, Jessica glanced at her notes from the

previous session. "Now, Zachary, I would like you to tell me more about the year you spent with your uncle in New Jersey."

Zachary sat in one of the two armchairs, facing the window. Since he seemed more comfortable speaking to her if he didn't have to look at her, Jessica had gotten into the habit of turning the chair away before ushering him in for his appointments.

"Nothing much to tell. My father ran out on my mom. She couldn't take care of me so she sent me to stay with her brother-in- law until she got back on her feet." Zachary tapped his foot in a rapid movement that Jessica had come to realize meant the question caused him discomfort.

"How did you get along with your uncle?"

"Okay, I guess." The tapping accelerated. "Did he have children of his own?" Zachary pulled his long legs up into the chair and wrapped his arms around his knees. "Yeah."

"And, how did you get along with them?" "Okay, I guess." "Did your uncle treat his own children differently than he treated you?" Jessica rose and stood behind Zachary's chair, stroking his long blond hair. If she was still seeing Zachary under supervision, she would get reprimanded for the physical contact. But, often she could use touch to calm him enough so he could verbalize his thoughts.

"He was a mean, ruthless, vicious, judgmental prick who seemed to get his kicks out of making me feel like I wasn't up to par with his own children. He kept pointing out how different and awkward I was. He always made it clear that I wasn't part of the family. He called me Zach even though I asked him not to." Zachary trembled like a heroin addict deep in withdrawal.

Jessica debated interrupting him, but he seemed so close to touching on something epiphanic. Despite the agitation his memories caused, she hated to stop him. She rubbed his shoulders, taken aback by the tension in his muscles.

"He had four kids, all of whom slowly became infected with his attitude of seeing me as some undesirable intruder into their home." Zachary fingers balled up into fists and his knuckles turned white. "I slept in a closet on the carpet with only a thin blanket. I couldn't wear my clothes to bed so I was always cold. He punished me for my lack of social skills by making me eat in the kitchen by myself while everyone else ate in the dining room. He would hit me so hard with his belt on my bare ass, he often broke skin. I had bruises on my arms from where he grabbed me, on my shins from where he kicked me."

Jessica leaned over the back of the chair and wrapped her arms across Zachary's chest. He grabbed onto her forearms, clinging to her.

She rested her cheek on the top of his head, offering comfort in her embrace to assuage the pain his memories would generate. "What else did he do to you, Zachary?"

His chest heaved and a sob escaped that sounded like a banshee's cry.

Jessica felt wet tears dripping onto her arm, but with Zachary on the verge of breakthrough, she kept pushing. "What else did he do to you, Zachary?"

"No, don't touch me." Zachary tore her arms from his chest and hurled himself under her desk.

His violence startled her and she had to grab the chair to keep from losing her balance, but Jessica wasn't willing to give up when he was so close to acknowledging what had happened in his childhood. She took a deep breath and walked over to the desk, leaned against the wall, and slid down so she squatted where he could see her face. "What else did he do to you, Zachary?"

Zachary curled up in a ball with this back toward her. His sobs shook his body so violently, Jessica worried he would hurt himself against the desk. Afraid she had pushed him too far, she crawled toward him, slowly put her arm under the desk and touched his hair. He didn't resist, but he didn't change position either. Nor did his sobbing abate.

"I think we've covered as much ground as we can today,

Zachary." Jessica kept her voice soft and soothing. She had to calm him down, she couldn't have him leaving her office in this state. "Why don't you come out from under the desk. We don't need to talk any more during this session."

He didn't react.

"Please come out from under there, Zachary. You'll feel better if you do." Jessica slid her hand from Zachary's hair along his arm until she reached his fingers. She tried to undo his fist enough so she could get a hold of his hand. Although he resisted at first, eventually his fingers relaxed and he allowed her to take his hand and tug on it.

When he crawled out from underneath the desk, Jessica pulled him into her arms and let him sob, shaking, with his face pressed against her shoulder. She stroked his hair and rocked him back and forth until he calmed down.

When his shaking stopped, she breathed a deep sigh of relief, but she didn't try to coax him to his feet until he stopped crying. Then she led him over to the chair and the box of tissues next to it. He blew his nose several times but ended up choking and she had to pat him on the back. Finally she got him to drink a glass of water and his hand remained steady while he did.

"Will you be okay going home?" He swallowed and nodded.

Z

Zachary missed his next two appointments and didn't answer his phone when Jessica tried to call him. After his second no-show, she debated whether she should call the police and have them check up on him. But of all her patients, he seemed the most likely candidate to test the Siberian research. One advantage he offered was his lack of a social network. If he disappeared for a few weeks, no one would notice. Creating a police file could create obstacles.

Jessica decided to pay Zachary a visit. She discovered he lived in a run-down structure that looked more like a hotel than an apartment building. The elevator had an "Out of Order" sign hanging from it and the stairs stank of urine. She debated about leaving, but in her six months at the clinic no other patient had presented such a perfect opportunity. Since she had read the rumors about Russian scientists in Siberia using whipping therapy to treat everything from drug addiction to depression, Jessica had wanted to do her own research. She knew she could never get anyone at the university or the clinic to endorse any kind of study and needed a patient she could persuade to let her try it.

After climbing the stairs, holding a handkerchief over her nose, Jessica had to bang on Zachary's door for almost ten minutes before he opened it. He reeked of sweat and unwashed clothing, several days of beard covered his face, his skin appeared pasty white, and he and looked like he had lost ten pounds.

"What?" He shaded his eyes from the light of the bare bulb in the hallway ceiling.

"You missed your appointment today."

"Ummm, I thought that was tomorrow. Sorry. I'll call and reschedule." He stepped back and pushed the door closed.

Jessica stuck her foot in the door. "You also missed your first appointment this week." She observed his emaciated form and bloodshot blue eyes. "When's the last time you ate?"

Zachary shrugged.

She pushed her way past him into the room despite his efforts to block her. Torn blue jeans and worn sweatshirts hung over two metal folding chairs. Empty take-out containers from a grocery store deli covered the card table that sat against one wall and the shelf that held a small microwave and a toaster oven. The unmade bed looked as if Zachary had climbed out of it to answer the door. A pile of magazines, the top one pornographic, sat next to the bed. Instead of a closet, the room had a rack attached to the wall next to the door. Another door, open next to the shelf, led to the bathroom. Even from this angle, Jessica could see how tiny it was.

"How long since you've left this room?" Jessica crossed her arms under her breasts, disgusted by the depths to which he had sunk.

Zachary shrugged.

"Have you gone anywhere since your last appointment?" He already had problems with late arrivals at work.

He shook his head.

Continue Reading

Shattered

Buy it in Print
978-1-937471-93-4
from Create Space

or Amazon
http://tinyurl.com/ShatteredPrint
or
E-Book
978-1-937471-92-7

www.ingramcontent.com/pod-product-compliance
Lightning Source LLC
Chambersburg PA
CBHW020643180626
46816CB00003B/1102